D0179496

Books by Robert B. Parker

THE GODWULF MANUSCRIPT
GOD SAVE THE CHILD
MORTAL STAKES
PROMISED LAND
THREE WEEKS IN SPRING
(with Joan Parker)
THE JUDAS GOAT
WILDERNESS
LOOKING FOR RACHEL WALLACE
EARLY AUTUMN
A SAVAGE PLACE
CEREMONY
THE WIDENING GYRE
LOVE AND GLORY
VALEDICTION
A CATSKILL EAGLE
TAMING A SEA-HORSE
PALE KINGS AND PRINCES
CRIMSON JOY

GOD SAVE
THE CHILD

Robert B. Parker

A DELL BOOK

Published by
Dell Publishing
a division of
The Bantam Doubleday Dell Publishing Group, Inc.
666 Fifth Avenue
New York, New York 10103

For information address: Delacorte Press/Seymour Lawrence,
New York, New York.
The trademark Dell® is registered in the U.S. Patent
and Trademark Office.
ISBN: 0-440-12899-4

Reprinted by arrangement with Delacorte Press/Seymour Lawrence

Printed in the United States of America

One Previous Edition

June 1987

10 9 8 7 6 5 4

KRI

*This is for
My Mother & Father*

1

If you leaned way back in the chair and cranked your neck hard over, you could see the sky from my office window, delft-blue and cloudless and so bright it looked solid. It was September after Labor Day, and somewhere the corn was probably as high as an elephant's eye, the kind of weather when a wino could sleep warm in a doorway.

"Mr. Spenser, are you listening to us?"

I straightened my head up and looked back at Roger and Margery Bartlett.

"Yes, ma'am," I said. "You were just saying about how you never dealt with a private detective before, but this was an extreme case and there seemed no other avenue. Everybody who comes in here tends to say about that same thing to me."

"Well it's true." She was probably older than she looked and not as heavy. Her legs were very slim, the kind women admire and men don't. They made her plumpish upper body look heavier. Her face had a bland, spoiled, pretty look, carefully made up with eye shadow and pancake makeup and false eyelashes. She looked as though if she cried she'd erode. Her hair, freshly blond, was cut close around her face. Gaminelike, I bet her hairdresser said. Mia Farrow, I bet he said. She was wearing a paisley caftan slit up the side and black, ankle-strapped platform shoes with three-inch soles and heels. Sitting opposite me, she had crossed her legs carefully so that the caftan fell away above the knee. I wanted to say, don't, your legs are too thin. But I knew she wouldn't believe me. She thought they were wonderful.

Just below her rib cage I could see the little bulge where her girdle stopped and the compressed flesh spilled over the top. She was wearing huge lavender sunglasses and lavender-dyed wooden beads on a leather thong. Authentic folk art, picked them up in Morocco on our last long weekend, the naïveté is charming, don't you think?

"We want you to find our son," she said.

"Okay."

"He's been gone a week. He ran away."

"Do you know where he might have run?" I asked.

"No," her husband answered. "I looked everywhere I could think of—friends, relatives, places he might hang out. I've asked everyone I know that knows him. He's gone."

"Have you notified the police?"

They both nodded. Mr. Bartlett said, "I talked to the chief myself. He says they'll do what they can, but of course it's a small force and there isn't much . . ."

He let his voice trail off and sat still and uncomfortable looking at me. He looked ill at ease in a shirt and tie. He was dressed in what must have been his wife's idea of the contemporary look. You can usually tell when a guy's wife buys his clothes. He had on baggy white cuffed flares, a solid scarlet shirt with long collar points, a wide pink tie, and a red-and-white-plaid seersucker jacket with wide lapels and the waist nipped. A prefolded handkerchief in his breast pocket matched the tie. He had on black and white saddle shoes and looked as happy as a hound in a doggie sweater. He should have been wearing coveralls and steel-toed work shoes. His hands looked strong and calloused, the nails were broken, and there was grime imbedded that the shower wouldn't touch.

"Why did he run away?" I asked.

"I don't know," Mrs. Bartlett answered. "He isn't a happy boy; he's going through some adolescent phase, I guess. Stays in his room most of the time. His grades are falling off. He used to get very good grades. He's very bright, you know."

"Why are you sure he ran away?" I didn't like asking the question.

Mr. Bartlett answered, "He took his guinea pig with him. Apparently he came home from school to get it and left."

"Did anyone see him leave?"

"No."

"Was anyone home when he came home?"

"No. I was at work and she was at her acting lessons."

"I take my acting lessons twice a week. In the afternoons. It's the only time I can get them. I'm a very creative person, you know, and I have to express myself."

Her husband said something that sounded like "umph."

"Besides," she said, "what has that got to do with anything? Are you saying if I'd been home he wouldn't have run off? Because that simply isn't so. Roger is hardly perfect, you know."

"I was asking because I was trying to find out if he snuck in and out or not. It might suggest whether he intended to run off when he came home."

"If I didn't express myself, I couldn't be as good a mother and wife. I do it for my family, mainly."

Roger looked like he'd just bitten his tongue.

"Okay," I said.

"Creative people simply must create. If you're not a creative person, you wouldn't understand."

"I know," I said. "I have the same damned problem. Right now for instance, I'm trying to create some information, and, for heaven's sake, I'm not getting anywhere at all."

Her husband said, "Yeah, will you for crissake, Marge, stop talking about yourself?"

She looked a little puzzled, but she shut up.

"Did the boy take anything besides the guinea pig?" I asked.

"No."

"Has he ever run away before?"

There was a long pause while they looked at each other. Then, like the punch line in a Frick-and-Frack routine, she said yes and he said no.

"That covers most of the possibilities," I said.

"He didn't really run away," Bartlett said. "He just slept over a friend's house without telling us. Any kid'll do that."

"He did not; he ran away," his wife said. She was intense and forgot about displaying her legs—the skirt slid over as she leaned forward and covered them entirely. "We called everywhere the next day, and Jimmy Houser's mother told us he'd been there. If you hadn't gone and got him at school, I don't think he'd have come back."

"Aw Marge, you make everything sound like a god-damned drama."

"Roger, there's something wrong with that kid, and you won't admit it. If you'd gone along with it when I wanted him looked at—but no, you were so worried about the money. 'Where am I going to get the money, Marge, do you think I've got a money tree in back, Marge?' If you'd let me take him someplace, he'd be home now."

The mimicry sounded true. Bartlett's tan face got darker.

"You bitch," he said. "I told you, take the money out of

your goddamned acting lessons and your goddamned
pottery classes and your goddamned sculpturing supplies
and your goddamned clothes. You got twenty years
psychology payments hanging in your goddamned
closet. . . ."

I was going to get a chance to check my erosion theory.
Tears began to well up in her eyes, and I found I didn't want
to check my theory nor did I want to see her erode. I put my
fingers in my ears and waited.

They stopped.

"Good," I said. "Now, let us establish some ground
rules. One, I am not on the Parent-of-the-Year committee. I
am not interested in assessing your performance. Yell at
each other when I'm not around. Second, I am a simple
person. If I'm looking for a lost kid, that's what I do. I don't
referee marriages; I don't act as creative consultant to the
Rog and Margie show. I just keep looking for the kid until I
find him. Third, I charge one hundred dollars a day plus
whatever expenses I incur. Fourth, I need five hundred
dollars as a retainer."

They were silent, embarrassed at the spillover I'd
witnessed.

Bartlett said, "Yeah, sure, that's okay, I mean hey, it's
only money, right? I'll give you a check now; I brought one
with me, in case, you know?"

He hunched the chair forward and wrote a check on the
edge of my desk with a translucent ballpoint pen. Bartlett
Construction was imprinted in the upper left corner of the
check—I was going to be a business expense. Deductible.
One keg of 8d nails, 500 feet of 2 x 4 utility grade, one
gumshoe, 100 gallons of creosote stain. I took the check
without looking at it and slipped it folded into my shirt
pocket, casual, like I got them all the time and it was just

something to pass along to my broker. Or maybe I'd buy some orchids with it.

"What is your first step?" Mrs. Bartlett said.

"I'll drive up to Smithfield after lunch and look at your house and look at his room and talk to teachers and the local fuzz and like that."

"But the police have done that. What can you do that they can't?" I wondered if I was cutting into her modern dance lessons.

"I can't do anything they can't, but I can do it full time. They have to arrest drunks and flag down speeders and break up fights at the high school and keep the kids from planting pot in the village watering trough. I don't. All I have to do is look for your kid. Also, maybe I'm smarter than they are."

"But can you find him?"

"I can find him; he's somewhere. I'll keep looking till I do."

They didn't look reassured. Maybe it was my office. If I was so good at finding things, how come I couldn't find a better office? Maybe I wasn't all that good? Maybe nobody is. I stood up.

"I'll see you this afternoon," I said. They agreed and left. I watched them from my window as they left the building and headed up Stuart Street toward the parking lot next to Jake Wirth's. An old drunk man with a long overcoat buttoned to his chin said something to them. They stared rigidly past him without answering and disappeared into the parking lot. Well, I thought, the rents are low. The old man stumbled on toward the corner of Tremont. He stopped and spoke to two hookers in hot pants and fancy hats. One of them gave him something, and he shuffled along. A blue

Dodge Club van pulled out of the parking lot and headed
down Stuart toward Kneeland Street and the expressway.
On the side it said Bartlett Construction. I could see one arm
in the sleeve of a paisley caftan on the window as it went by.

2

I drove north out of Boston over the Mystic River Bridge with the top down on my car. On the right was Old Ironsides at berth in the Navy Yard and to the left of the bridge the Bunker Hill Monument. Between them stretch three-decker tenements alternating with modular urban renewal units. One of the real triumphs of prefab design is to create a sense of nostalgia for slums. At the top of the bridge I paid my toll to a man who took pride in his work. There was a kind of precise flourish to the way he took my quarter and gave me back a dime with the same hand.

Out to the right now was the harbor and the harbor islands and the long curving waterfront. The steeple of the Old North Church poked up among the warehouses and lofts. On the East Boston side of the harbor was Logan Airport and beyond, northeast, the contours of the coast. The brick and asphalt and neon were blurred by distance and sunshine, and beneath it I got a sense of the land as it once must have been. The silent midsummer buzz of it and copper-colored near-naked men moving along a narrow trail.

The bridge dipped down into Chelsea and the Northeast Expressway. Across the other lane beyond a football field was a Colonel Sanders' fast-food restaurant. The brick and asphalt and neon were no longer blurred, and the sense of the land went away. The expressway connects in Saugus to Route 1 and for the next ten miles is a plastic canyon of sub-sandwich shops, discount houses, gas stations, supermarkets, neocolonial furniture shops (vinyl siding and chintz curtains), fried chicken, big beef sandwiches, hot dogs cooked in beer, quarter-pound hamburgers, pizzas, storm doors, Sears, Roebuck and Co., doughnut shops, stockade fencing—preassembled sections, restaurants that look like log cabins, restaurants that look like sailing ships, restaurants that look like Moorish town houses, restaurants that look like car washes, car washes, shopping centers, a fish market, a skimobile shop, an automotive accessory shop, liquor stores, a delicatessen in three clashing colors, a motel with an in-room steam bath, a motel with a relaxing vibrator bed, a car dealer, an indoor skating rink attractively done in brick and corrugated plastic, a trailer park, another motel composed of individual cabins, an automobile dealership attractively done in glass and corrugated plastic, an enormous steak house with life-sized plastic cows grazing out front in the shadow of a six-story neon cactus, a seat cover store, a discount clothing warehouse, an Italian restaurant with a leaning tower attached to it. Overpasses punctuate Route 1, tying together the north suburban towns that line it like culverts over a sewer of commerce. Maybe Squanto had made a mistake.

A sign said Entering Smithfield, and the land reappeared. There was grass along the highway and maple trees behind it and glimpses of lake through the trees. I turned off at an exit marked Smithfield and drove toward the center of town beneath a tunnel of elm trees that were as old as the town. They bordered the broad street and interlaced thirty feet above it so that the sun shone through in mottled patterns on the street. Bordering the street behind big lawns and flowering shrubs were spacious old houses in shingle or clapboard, often with slate roofs, occasionally with small

barns that had been converted to garages. Stone walls, rose
bushes, red doors with bull's-eye glass windows, a lot of
station wagons, most of them with the fake wood on the
sides. I was more aware than I had been of the big dent on
the side of my car and the tear in the upholstery that I had
patched with gray tape.

In the center of town was a common with a two-story
white clapboard meeting house in the middle. The date on it
was 1681. Across the street was a white spired church with
a big church hall attached and next to that a new white
clapboard library designed in harmony with the meeting
house and church. On a stone wall across from the common
six teenage kids, four boys and two girls, sat swinging their
bare feet and smoking. They were long-haired and T-shirted
and tan. I turned right onto Main Street at the end of the
common and then left. A discreet white sign with black
printing on it was set in a low curving brick wall. It said
Apple Knoll.

It was a development. Flossy and fancy and a hundred
thousand a house, but a development. Some of the trees had
been left and the streets curved gently and the lawns were
well landscaped, but all the homes were the same age and
bore the mark of a central intelligence. They were big
colonial houses, some garrisoned, some with breezeways,
some with peaked and some with gambrel roofs, but
basically the same house. Eight or ten rooms, they looked to
be, on an acre of land. Behind the houses on my right the
land sloped down to a lake that brightened through the trees
here and there where the road bent closer.

The Bartletts' home was yellow with dark green shutters
and a hip roof. The roof was slate, and there were A-shaped
dormers protruding from it to suggest a third floor that was
more than attic. Doubtless for the servants: they don't mind
the heat under the eaves; they're used to it.

A brick walk led up to a wide green front door with sidelights. The brick driveway went parallel to the house and curved right, ending in a turnaround before a small barn designed like the house and done in the same colors. The blue van was there and a Ford Country Squire and a red Mustang convertible with a white roof and a black Chevrolet sedan with a buggy-whip antenna and no markings on the side.

The barn doors were open and swallows flew in and out in sharp, graceful sweeps. Behind the house was a square swimming pool surrounded by a brick patio. The blue lining of the pool made the water look artificial. Beyond the pool a young girl was operating a ride-around lawn mower. I parked next to the black Chevy, up against the hydrangea bushes that lined the turnaround and concealed it from the street. Black-and-yellow bumblebees buzzed frantically at the flowers. As I approached the house, a Labrador retriever looked at me without raising his head from his paws, and I had to walk around him to get to the back door. Somewhere out of sight I could hear an air conditioner droning, and I was conscious of how my shirt stuck to my back under my coat. I was wearing a white linen sport coat in honor of my trip to the subs, and I wished I could take it off. But since I'd made some people in the mob mad at me, I'd taken to wearing a gun everywhere, and Smithfield didn't seem like the kind of place where you flashed it around.

Besides the white linen jacket, I had on a red checkered sport shirt, dark blue slacks, and white loafers. Me and Betsy Ross. I was neat, clean, alert, and going to the back door. I rang the bell. Ding-dong, private eye calling.

Roger Bartlett came to the door looking more comfortable but no happier than when I'd last seen him. He had on blue sneakers and Bermuda shorts and a white sleeveless undershirt. He had a glass of what looked like gin and tonic in his hand and, from the smell of his breath, several more in his stomach.

"C'mon in, c'mon in," he said. "How about something to fight the heat, maybe a cold one or two, a little schnapps? Hey, why not?" He made a two-inch measuring gesture with his thumb and forefinger as he backed into the kitchen, and I followed. It was a huge kitchen with a big maple-stained trestle table in the bay of the back windows. A cop was sitting at the table with Margery Bartlett, drinking a sixteen-ounce can of Narragansett beer. He had a lot of gold braid on his shoulders and sleeves and more on the visored cap that lay beside him on the table. He had a pearl-handled forty-five in a black holster on a Sam Browne belt. The belt made a gully in his big stomach and the short-sleeved dark blue uniform shirt stretched very tight across his back. It was soaked with sweat around the armpits and along the spine. His bare arms were sunburned and almost hairless, and his big round face was fiery red with pale circles around his eyes where his sunglasses protected him. He'd recently had a haircut, and a white line circled each ear. His eyes were very pale blue and quite small, and he had hardly any neck, his head seeming to grow out of his shoulders. He took a long pull on the beer and belched softly.

"I'll take a can of beer," I said.

Bartlett got one from the big poppy-red refrigerator. "Want a glass?"

"No, thank you."

The kitchen was paneled in pale gray boards, the counter tops were three-inch maple chopping blocks, the cabinets were red and so were the appliances. The wall opposite the big bow window was brick, and the appliances were built into it. An enormous copper hood spread out over the stove, and on the brick wall hung copper pans which bore no marks of use.

The floor was square flagstone, gray and red, and a hand-braided blue and red oval rug covered much of it. There were captain's chairs around the table and some reddish maple barstools along the counter. I sat on one and popped open the beer.

Margery Bartlett said, "Mr. Spenser, this is Chief Trask of our police force. He's been working on the case." Her voice was a little loud, and as she spoke she held her empty glass out toward her husband. Trask nodded at me. Bartlett filled his wife's glass from a half-gallon bottle of Beefeater gin on the counter, added a slice of lime, some ice, and some Schweppes tonic, and put it down in front of her.

Trask said, "I'd like to get a few things out in the open early, Spenser."

"Candor," I said, "complete candor. It's the only way."

He stared at me without speaking for a long while. Then he said, "Is that a wise remark, boy?" At thirty-seven I wasn't too used to being called boy.

"No, sir," I said. "Anyone who knows me will tell you that I'm really into candor. Only don't give me that hard look anymore; it makes it hard to swallow my beer."

"Keep it up, Spenser, and you'll see how hard things can get. Understand?"

I drank some more beer. It's one of the things I'm outstanding at. I said, "Okay, what was it you wanted to get out in the open?"

He kept the hard stare on me. "I did some checking with a few people I know in the AG's office, after Rog told me he'd hired you. And I found out some things I don't like hearing."

"I'll bet," I said.

"Among them is that you think you're kind of fancy and act like you're kind of special. You don't always cooperate with local authorities, they said."

"Jesus, I was hoping that wouldn't get out," I said.

"Well, let me tell you something right now, Mister; out here in Smithfield you'll cooperate. You'll keep in close touch with my department, and you'll be under the supervision of my people, or you'll be hauling your ass— excuse me, Marge—right back into Boston. You got that?"

"How long you been working on that stare?" I said.

"Huh?"

"I mean, do you work out with it every morning in the mirror? Or is it something that once you've mastered it you never forget, like, say, riding a bicycle?"

Trask brought his open hand down hard on the tabletop. The ice in Margery Bartlett's glass jingled. She said, "George, please."

"This isn't getting us nowhere, you know? This isn't getting us nowhere at all," Roger Bartlett said. Outside I could hear the low murmur of the power mower as it trimmed up the far side of the acre.

Trask took a deep forbearing breath and said, "Gimme another beer, will you, Rog?"

Bartlett did and put down another can by me, although I wasn't halfway through the first one.

I said, "What have you got, Chief?"

"Everything there is to get; we've covered everything. The kid has run off and there's no way to find him. I say he's probably in New York or maybe California by now."

"Why do you say that?"

"Because he's not around here. If he was we'd have found him." Trask drank again from the can.

"What did he take when he left?"

"Just a pet whatchamacallit," Margery Bartlett said. "Guinea pig."

"Yeah," Trask said, "guinea pig. He took that and what

he was wearing and nothing else. Haven't the Bartletts told you all this?"

"What was he wearing?"

"Blue short-sleeved shirt, tan pants, white sneakers."

"Did he take any food for the guinea pig?"

Trask looked at me as if I were crazy. "Food?"

"Yeah. Food. Did he take any for the guinea pig?"

Trask looked at Margery Bartlett. She said, "I don't know. I had nothing to do with the guinea pig." She shivered. "Dirty little things. I hate them."

I looked at her husband. He shook his head. "I don't know."

"What goddamned difference does that make? We ain't worrying about the whatchamacallit; we're after a missing kid. I don't care if the whatchamacallit eats well or not."

"Well," I said, "if the kid cared enough about the guinea pig to come home and get it before taking off, he wouldn't. have left without food for it, would he? How about a carrying case or a box or something?"

All three of them looked blank.

"Did the shirt he was wearing have a big pocket, big enough for a guinea pig?"

Roger Bartlett said, "No, I put it through the wash the day before he left, and I noticed there were no pockets. I always go through the pockets before I put things in the wash, ya know, because the kids are always sticking things in their pockets and then forgetting them and they get ruined in the machine. So I checked and I noticed, ya know?"

"Okay," I said, "let's see if we can figure out whether he took any food or anything to carry the guinea pig. If you're going to New York or California, you probably don't want to carry a guinea pig in your hand the whole way. You can't put him in your pants pocket, and you probably don't buy him a cheeseburger and a Ho-Jo at Howard Johnson's."

Roger Bartlett nodded and said, "Come on."

We went up through a center hall off the kitchen to the front stairs. The stairs were wide enough to drive a jeep up. Where they turned and formed a landing, a floor-to-ceiling window looked out over the bright blue pool. There was a trumpet vine fringing the window, and its big bugle-shaped red flowers obscured a couple of the window lights.

The boy's room was second floor front, looking out over the broad front lawn and the quiet curving street beyond it. The bed was against the far wall, a low, headboardless affair that the stores insist on calling a Hollywood bed. It was covered with a red and black spread. There was a matching plaid rug on the floor and drapes of the same material as the spread on the windows. To the left of the door as we entered the room was a built-in counter that covered the entire wall. Beneath it were bureau drawers, and atop it were books and paper and some pencils and a modular animal cage of clear plastic with an orange plastic base. There was a water bottle still nearly full in its slot and some food in the dish. The perforated metal cover was open, and the cage was empty. Beside the cage was a cardboard box with the cover on. Bartlett opened the box. Inside was a package of guinea pig food pellets, a package of Guinea Pig Treat, and a blue cardboard box with a carry handle and a yellow picture of a satisfied-looking guinea pig on the outside.

Bartlett said, "That box is what they give you at the pet store to bring them home in. Kevin kept it to carry him around in."

The two packages of food, both open, and the carry box occupied all the space in the shoe box.

I said, "Can you tell if there's any food missing?"

"I don't think so. This is where he kept it, and it's still there."

I stared around the room. It was very neat. A pair of

brown loafers was lined up under the bed, and a pair of blue canvas bedroom slippers beside them, geometrically parallel. The bedside table had a reading lamp and a small red portable radio and nothing else. At the far end of the counter top was a brown and beige portable TV set. Neatly on top, one edge squared with the edge of the television, was a current *TV Guide*. I opened the closet door. The clothes were hung in precise order, each item on its hanger, each shirt buttoned up on the hanger, the pants each neatly creased on a pants hanger; a pair of Frye boots was the only thing on the floor.

"Who does his room?" I asked.

"He does," his father said. "Isn't he neat? Never saw a kid as neat as he is. Neat as a bastard, ya know?"

I nodded and began to look through the bureau drawers. They were as neat as the rest of the room. Folded underwear, rolled socks, six polo shirts of different colors with the sleeves neatly folded under. Two of the drawers were entirely empty.

"What was in these drawers?" I asked.

"Nothing, I think. I don't think he ever kept anything in there."

"Are you sure?"

"No. Like I say, he kept care of his own room, mostly."

"How about your wife; would she know?"

"No."

"Okay." I looked around the room in case there was a secret panel or a note written in code and scratched on the window with the edge of a diamond. I saw neither. In fact there was nothing else in the room. No pictures on the wall, no nude pictures, no pot, no baseballs autographed by Carl Yastrzemski. It was like the sample rooms that furniture departments put up in big department stores: neat, symmetrical, color-coordinated, and empty.

"What are you looking for?" Bartlett asked me.

"Whatever's here," I said. "I don't know until I see it."

"Well, you through?"

"Yeah," I said, and we went back downstairs.

When we came back to the kitchen, Trask was at the counter mixing another gin and tonic for Marge Bartlett. There were two more empty half-quart cans before his empty chair at the table, and Marge Bartlett's voice had gotten louder.

"Well, we put it on in front of a group of young high school kids out in Bolton," she was saying, "and the reception was fantastic. If you give children a chance to see creative drama, they'll respond."

Trask belched, less softly than he had the last time. " 'Scuse *me*, Marge," he said.

"Lotta gas in that 'Gansett," Roger Bartlett said. "It's a real gassy beer. I don't know why I buy it; it's really gassy, ya know?"

Bartlett made himself another gin and tonic as he spoke. I opened my second can of beer and swallowed a little. Gassy, I thought.

Marge Bartlett got up and bumped her hip against the table as she did. She crossed the kitchen toward me with an unlighted cigarette in her mouth and said quite close to my face, "Gotta match?"

I said, "No." She was leaning her thighs against me as I sat on the barstool, and the smell of gin was quite strong. I wondered if the gin was gassy too. She looked at me out of the corners of her eyes with her eyelids dropped down so her eyes were just slits and spoke to her husband.

"Why don't you have shoulders like Mr. Spenser, Rog? I bet he looks great with his shirt off. Do you look great with your shirt off, Mr. Spenser?" Her unlit cigarette bobbed up and down in her mouth as she talked.

"Yeah, but I usually wear one because my tommy gun tends to cut into my skin when I don't."

She looked puzzled for a minute, but then Trask held a flaming Zippo lighter at her, and she got her cigarette going, took a big inhale and exhale through her nose without taking the cigarette out. She squeezed my upper arm with her right hand and said, "Oooooh." I said, "Seen many Marlene Dietrich movies lately?"

That puzzled look again. She stepped back and picked up her drink. "I have to wee wee," she said. And made what I guess was a seductive move toward the bathroom. I finished my beer.

"You spot anything, Sherlock Holmes?" Trask said.

I shook my head.

Trask looked pleased. "I didn't think you would," he said. "We're not a big force, but we're trained in modern techniques and we're highly disciplined."

"I think the kid's local, though," I said. "Or he went with someone."

"The hell you say."

"He wouldn't set out for a long trip with a guinea pig in his hand and no food, no carry case, not even a spacious pocket. He might run in from a waiting car and grab the guinea pig and run out again. He'd go a short ride carrying the guinea pig, but not a long one. He's a neat kid; everything is laid out in squares and angles. He wouldn't be so unneat as to forget food and lodging for the guinea pig."

"Hey, that's right," Bartlett said. "He would never have done that; Kevin wasn't like that; he'd never have gone off like that unless he was going like you say, Spenser. He'd never do that."

Somewhere off the kitchen a toilet flushed and a door opened and a minute later Marge Bartlett reappeared.

"Spenser thinks Kevin's around here somewhere," Bartlett said to her. "That he wouldn't have gone far without taking stuff for the guinea pig and some clothes and things."

She drained the rest of her drink and gestured the glass indiscriminately at the room. Trask jumped up. "I'll get it, Marge. Sit still, Rog, I got it."

"How does that sound to you, Mrs. Bartlett?" I asked. "Is Kevin the kind of kid to go off that way without preparation?"

"Marge," she said. "Call me Marge."

Trask gave her a fresh drink and helped himself to another beer from the refrigerator.

Bartlett said, "Jeez, I better slice up some more limes; gin and tonic without limes is like a kiss without a squeeze, right? I mean without a goddamned lime it's like a kiss without a squeeze."

Marge Bartlett popped another cigarette into her mouth. It had floral designs on it. Trask leaned over with his Zippo and lit it. The Zippo had a Marine Corps world and anchor emblem on it. I bet he hadn't had the stomach thirty years ago at Parris Island.

"Is he, Marge?" I asked.

"Is he what?" she said.

"Is he the kind of kid that would go off without making any provisions for anything? His room doesn't look like the room of that kind of person."

"That's right. He's just like his damned father. So careful, so neat. Everything has to be the same. Not like me at all; I'm spontaneous. 'Spontaneous Me.' Ever read that poem? By Whittier?"

"Whitman," I said.

"Yes, excuse me, Whitman, of course. Anyway, I'm spontaneous, spur-of-the-moment, zip-zap, go anywhere, do anything. Most creative people are like that, I guess, but not Kevin; a stick-in-the-mud just like old Roger Stick-in-the-mud. Supper's got to be at six, plain food, roast beef, baked beans. I'd cook if they'd eat something creative, Julia Child, that kind of thing, but it's got to be the same old stew, steak, hamburg. The hell with them; let them cook it themselves. Now if they would eat veal steak in wine with cherries . . ."

"My ass," Bartlett said. "You're not creative, you're lazy. You haven't cooked a goddamned meal around here in five years. Veal with my ass."

"Hey, Rog," Trask said. "Now there's no way to talk. Marge has put out a wonderful feed at parties and stuff."

"Yeah, catered from the goddamned deli for half my freaking profits for the month."

"Oh, you sonova bitch," Marge said. "That's all you think about is your money. If you think I can take acting lessons and modern dance and sculpting all day long and try to keep myself young and interesting for you and the children and then come home and prepare a party that you'll be proud of . . ."

"Balls," Bartlett said, his face very red now. "You don't give a rat's ass about me or anybody else."

"Hold on now," Trask said. "Goddamn it, just hold on."

I got off my barstool and took another can of beer out of the refrigerator. You don't see red refrigerators much. I went to the back door and opened it and went out. The retriever still lay there on the back steps with his tongue out, and I sat down beside him and opened the beer. The door behind me was on a pneumatic closer, and as it shut I heard Marge Bartlett say "shit" in a very loud voice.

I drank a small swallow of the beer and scratched the dog's ear. His tail thumped on the porch. The sound of the lawn mower stopped, and a minute later a young girl came out of the barn and walked toward the house. She didn't look at me sitting on the back steps but detoured toward the front of the house, and a minute later I heard the front door open and close.

I drank some more beer. In the middle of the front lawn, past the hydrangea, was a huge flowering crab. It was too late for blossoms, but the leaves were still reddish fading into green, and there were small green crab apples beginning to form. Some robins and some sparrows and a Baltimore oriole swarmed in and out of the branches with considerable chatter. After the green fruit, I supposed. I hadn't seen a Baltimore oriole since I was a kid.

I heard the front door open and close again, and the girl came around the corner of the house wearing a bikini bathing suit and carrying a towel. She must have been thirteen or fourteen and was just beginning to get a figure. I was very careful not to lech at her. There has to be a line you won't cross, and my lower limit is arbitrarily set at sixteen. As she walked by she looked at the ground and said nothing. I watched her as she went around the corner of the house toward the pool. The retriever got up as she passed and followed her. They were out of sight, and then I heard two splashes in the pool. And the sound of swimming. My beer was gone. I looked at my watch; nearly four thirty. I put the beer can on the railing of the porch, walked across the driveway, got in my car, and drove back to Boston.

3

At eight the next morning I was out jogging along the Charles. From the concert shell on the Esplanade to the BU Bridge was two miles, and I always tried to make the round trip in about forty minutes. It was never fun, but this morning was tougher than usual because it was raining like hell. Usually there were other joggers, but this morning I was alone. I had on sweat pants and a hooded nylon shell, but the rain soaked my sneakers and needled at my face as I ran. Walking back up Arlington Street to my apartment on Marlborough, I could feel the sweat collect in the small of my back, trapped there by the waterproof parka.

Before I'd left I'd put the coffee on, and it was ready when I came back. But I didn't drink it yet. First a shower. A long time under the shower, a lot of soap, a lot of shampoo. I shaved very carefully, standing in the shower— I'd put a mirror in the stall just so I could do that—and rinsed off thoroughly. I put on a pair of light gray slacks and black over-the-ankle boots and went to the kitchen.

I sliced two green tomatoes, sprinkled them with black pepper and rosemary, shook them in flour, and put them in about a half-inch of olive oil to fry. I put a small porterhouse steak under the broiler and got a loaf of unleavened Syrian bread out of the refrigerator. While the steak and tomatoes cooked, I drank my first cup of coffee, cream, two sugars and ate a bowl of blackberries I'd bought at a farm stand coming back from the Cape with a girl I knew. When it was ready, I ate my breakfast, put the dishes in the washer, washed my hands and face, clipped my gun on over my right hip pocket, put on a washed blue denim shirt with short sleeves, and let it hang outside to cover the gun. I was ready, exercised, washed, fed, and armed—alert for the slightest sign of a dragon. I had a white trench coat given me once by a friend. She said it made me look taller. I put it on now and headed for my car.

The rain was hard as I pulled out onto Storrow Drive and headed for Smithfield. The wipers were only barely able to stay ahead of it, and some of the storm culverts were flooded and backing up in the underpasses.

I stopped at a white colonial liquor store in Smithfield Center and got directions to the high school. It was a little out from the center of town in a neighborhood of expensive homes with a football field behind it and some tennis courts beyond that. A sign said Visitors' Parking, and I slid in between an orange Volvo and a blue Pinto station wagon. I turned the collar up on my trench coat, got out of the car, and sprinted for the front doorway.

Inside was an open lobby with display cases on the walls containing graphics done by students. To the left was a glassed-in room with a sign on the door saying Administration and a smaller sign beneath saying Reception. I went in and spoke to a plump middle-aged lady with a tight permanent. I asked to see the principal.

"He's at conference this morning," she said. "Perhaps the assistant principal, Mr. Moriarty, can help you."

I said that Mr. Moriarty would be fine. She asked my name and disappeared into another office. She returned in a moment and gestured me in.

Mr. Moriarty was red-faced, swag-bellied, thick-necked

Irish. He was wearing a dark blue sharkskin suit with natural shoulders and narrow lapels, a white shirt with button-down collar, and a thin black knit tie.

Cordovan shoes, I thought, not wing tips; plain-toed cordovan shoes and white socks. I wished there were someone there to bet with. He stood up behind his desk as I came in and put out his hand.

"I'm Mr. Moriarty, the assistant principal," he said. We shook hands.

His hair was brown and surprisingly long, cut square in a kind of Dutch-boy bob across the forehead, completely covering his ears, and waving over his shirt collar. Modish. I gave him my card. He read it and raised his eyebrows.

"Private investigator. Hey, I was an MP, you know. In Germany after the war, stationed in Stuttgart," he said.

I said, "I'm looking into the disappearance of one of your students, Kevin Bartlett. I was wondering if you could tell me anything about him that might help."

Moriarty frowned. "We've been through all that with Chief Trask," he said. "I don't know what I could add to what I told him."

"Let's go over what you told him," I said. "Sometimes a fresh slant can help."

"Does Chief Trask know you are here? I mean, I don't want to get into some conflict of ethics on this. Chief Trask is, after all, the—um—well—the chief."

"He knows, and I won't ask you to compromise your ethics. Just tell me about the kid."

"Well, he's quite a bright student. Good family, father runs a successful contracting firm. Good family, been in town a long time, beautiful home up in Apple Knoll."

"I know," I said. "I've been there, but I'm more interested in information about the kid. What kind of kid was he? Was he any kind of behavior problem? Did he have many friends? Who were they? What were they like? Was he using drugs? Did he drink? Did he have a girl friend? Was there a teacher he was close to? Why would he run off? That sort of thing. I'm glad he was from a good family, you understand; I'd just like to see about getting him back to it."

"Well, that's a big order," Moriarty said. "And I question whether or not I'm authorized to discuss these matters with you."

"Just 'whether,'" I said.

"I beg your pardon?" he said.

"'Whether' implies 'or not,'" I said.

His professional manner slipped a little. "Listen," he said, "I don't need my grammar corrected by some damned gumshoe. And I don't have to tell you anything at all. You think I've got all day to sit around and talk, you got another think coming."

"You've got a real way with the language," I said. "But, never mind, I'm not here to fight with you. I'm looking for help. Was the kid ever in trouble?"

"Well, sometimes he got a little insolent, especially with the women teachers. He has only been up here a year. This is just the start of his second year here, and we don't have a lot of experience with him. You might want to talk with Mr. Lee down at the junior high." He looked at his watch. "Or perhaps while you're here you might want to talk with Mrs. Silverman of our guidance department. She might be able to tell you something."

Good going, Spenser. Insult the guy's grammar so he sulks at you and won't talk. Maybe I ought to watch my mouth as people keep telling me. Moriarty was up from his desk and walking me to the door. I glanced down. Right! Plain-toed cordovans. Not shined. White socks too. Perfect.

"Mrs. Silverman's office is third door down this corridor

on the right. The door says Guidance on it, and you can't miss it."

I said thank you and went where he pointed me. There were lockers along the right-hand wall and doors with frosted-glass windows in them on my left. On the third one was lettered Guidance. I went in. It was like the waiting room at a doctor's office. Low table in the center, a rack for periodicals on one wall, a receptionist opposite, and three doors on the left wall like examining rooms. The periodical rack was filled with college catalogues, and the low table had literature about careers and health on it. The receptionist was a great improvement on Moriarty's. She had red hair and a dark tan and a lot of good-sized bosom showing over and around a lime-green sleeveless blouse. I told her Mr. Moriarty had sent me down to talk with Mrs. Silverman.

"She has a student with her now. Could you wait a moment please?"

I picked up some of the career leaflets on the table. Nursing, Air Force, G.E. Apprentice Training; I wondered if they had one for Private Eye. I looked. They didn't. The door to Mrs. Silverman's office opened, and a thin boy with shoulder-length hair and acne came out.

He mumbled, "Thank you, Mrs. Silverman," and hustled out of the office.

The secretary and her bosom got up and went into the office. In a moment they came out, and she said, "Mrs. Silverman will see you now."

I put down my copy of *Opportunities in Civil Service* and went in. Susan Silverman wasn't beautiful, but there was a tangibility about her, a physical reality, that made the secretary with the lime-green bosom seem insubstantial. She had shoulder-length black hair and a thin dark Jewish face with prominent cheekbones. Tall, maybe five seven, with black eyes. It was hard to tell her age, but there was a sense about her of intelligent maturity which put her on my side of thirty.

She said, "Come in, Mr. Spenser. I'm Susan Silverman," and came around the desk to shake hands. She was wearing a black silk blouse with belled sleeves and white slacks. The blouse was open at the throat, and there was a thin silver chain around her neck. Her breasts were good, her thighs were terrific. When she shook hands with me, I felt something click down back of my solar plexus.

I said hello without stammering and sat down.

"Why don't you take off your coat?" she said.

"Well, it's supposed to make me look taller," I said.

"Sitting down?"

"No, I guess not," I said and stood up and took it off. She took it from me and hung it on a rack beside hers. Hers was white too, and the two coats overlapped on the rack. It wasn't much, but it was a start.

"I don't think you need to look taller, Mr. Spenser," she said. When she smiled the color of her face seemed to heighten. "How tall are you?"

"Six one," I said.

"Really? That's surprising. I must admit you don't look that tall."

"Even with the raincoat?" I said.

"Even with that," she said. "You're so wide. Do you work with weights?"

"Yeah, some. How could you tell? Your husband lift?"

"Ex-husband," she said. "Yes, he played tackle for Harvard and stayed with the weights afterward."

Ex-husband! I felt the click again. She wasn't wearing a wedding ring. She had red polish on her fingernails and a thin silver bracelet around her left wrist. Small coiled earrings matched the bracelet and necklace. Her eyes had a dusting of blue shadow, and her lipstick matched the nail polish. Her teeth were very even and white, slightly prominent. Her hair was shiny and done in what we called a pageboy when I was in high school. There was just the slightest suggestion of laugh lines around her mouth.

"What can I do for you, Mr. Spenser?" she asked, and I realized I'd been staring at her.

"I'm trying to find Kevin Bartlett," I said and handed her one of my cards. "Mr. Moriarty suggested you might be able to tell me something about him."

"Have you talked to Mr. Moriarty already?" she said.

"In a manner of speaking. He seemed a little cautious."

"Yes, he is. Public school administrators are often cautious. What did he tell you about Kevin?"

"That he came from a good family and lived in a nice house."

"That's all?"

"Yeah. I think I offended him."

"Why?"

"Because he pouted and stamped his foot and sent me down here."

She laughed. Her laugh sounded like I'd always imagined the taste of mead. It was resonant.

"You must have teased him," she said.

"Well, a little.'

"Arthur does not respond well to teasing. But, about Kevin," she said. "Do you want to ask me questions, or do you want me to hold forth on what I know and think?"

"You hold forth," I said.

"Have you met Kevin's parents? You must have."

"Yes."

"What do you think?"

"Bad. Role identity is screwed up, no real communication. Probably a lot more than that, but I only met them twice. I think they probably drink too much."

"Okay. I've met them several times and we agree. Kevin's a product of that. He's a very intelligent kid, but he too has his roles tangled. And, at fifteen, going through adolescence, he still hasn't resolved his Oedipal conflicts. He's got some problems, I think, with gender identification, and strong problems of hostility toward both parents for different reasons."

"Are you suggesting he's homosexual?" I asked.

"No, not necessarily, but I think he could go that way. A dominant, but largely absent mother, a successful, but essentially passive father. Strength seems associated with femininity, resentful submission with masculinity, and love, perhaps, with neither."

"I have the feeling I'm only getting a piece of what you're saying," I said. "Is it too much of an oversimplification for me to say that because his parents are as they are, he's not sure whether he'd prefer to be like his mother or like his father when he gets to be an adult?"

She smiled a luminous smile and said, "That will do. One thing, though; this is only an opinion and one based on not enough data. I think I'm right, but I have a master's degree in guidance; I am not a psychiatrist."

"Okay, go ahead. What else can you tell me?"

"He moves with a really damaging group for a boy like him."

"Troublemakers?"

"No, not in the usual sense. Dropouts would be a better word. He has few friends in school. He spends most of his time with a group who have dropped out of school. Their approach to life is asocial if not antisocial, and for a boy with unresolved Oedipal hostilities it seems the worst possible choice of companions."

"Do you think he might be with one of this group?"

"Yes."

"Do you have an idea which?"

"No. That I can't be sure of. Kevin is not very talkative. He's been to see me a couple of times. He has difficulties with the women teachers. Nothing that is easily explained, but a kind of nagging hostility which is difficult to deal with."

"For instance?"

"Oh, telling one of the younger teachers she looks sexy. If she reprimands him he'll say, okay, you don't look sexy. That sort of thing. There's nothing really you can discipline him for, and indeed, to do so makes you look more ridiculous. He's very clever that way."

"Okay, can you give me an idea of this group he hangs with?"

"Well, as I say, he's not communicative, and he's very clever. When I've talked with him, I've learned that he has friends among the local dissidents, I suppose you'd call them, and he seems particularly friendly with someone named Vic Harroway. But who or where he is I don't know. I'm not close to the situation. Kevin is only one of maybe twenty kids a day I talk with."

"All with problems?"

"No, not emotional ones. Some of them just want advice on where to go to college, or when to take the college boards, or how to get a job as a bulldozer operator. But four or five a day are emotional problems, and there isn't time, nor have I sufficient training, really, to help them. The best I can do is recommend help at one or another guidance clinic and give the name of some psychotherapists I trust."

"Did you suggest that to Kevin's parents?"

"Well, I asked them to come and talk with me, but they never came. And I didn't want to just send them a letter suggesting it. So I did not make any recommendation."

"How did you ask them? I mean, did you write a letter or

see them at PTA or send a note home with Kevin? Or
what?"

"I called Mrs. Bartlett and asked if she and her husband
could come in. She said yes and we made an appointment,
but they never came. Why do you want to know?"

"Because it's there. Because it's better to know than not
to know in my line of work.'

She smiled, her teeth very white in her dark face.

"Maybe in all lines of work," she said. And I was proud
that I'd said a smart thing.

4

The rain had stopped when I left Susan Silverman and headed back for the Bartletts' house. I wanted to see what they could tell me about their son's social circle. If there was a group like that around, it would be a fair bet he'd go to it. Smithfield didn't look like the spot for a commune. But then, I wasn't quite sure what a spot for a commune looked like.

When I pulled into the Bartlett driveway, the chief's car was there again along with three others. One was a cream-colored Thunderbird with a black vinyl roof. One was a blue Ford station wagon with Smithfield Police lettered in black on the sides and the emergency number 555-3434 across the back. The third was a two-tone powder-blue and dark blue Massachusetts State Police cruiser. A state cop with a uniform that matched the cruiser and a gray campaign hat was leaning against it with his arms folded. The short-sleeved blue shirt was pressed with military creases; the black shoes were spit-shined. The campaign hat was tipped forward over the bridge of his nose like a Parris Island DI's. He had a big-handled Magnum .357 on a shiny black belt. He looked at me with no expression on his tanned and healthy face as I got out of my car.

"May I have your name, sir?" he said.

"Spenser," I said. "I'm working for the Bartletts. What's going on?"

"Do you have any identification, please," he said.

I fumbled under my sport coat for my wallet, and as I brought it out, the Magnum .357 was suddenly right up against my neck, and the cop said very seriously, "Put both hands on the top of the car, you sonova bitch." I put my hands, the wallet still clutched in the left one, on the top of my car and leaned.

"What's the matter," I said. "Don't you like my name?"

With his left hand he reached under my jacket and took my gun from the holster.

"Not bad," I said. "You must have gotten just a flash of it when I took out my wallet."

"Now the wallet," he said.

I handed it to him without ceasing to lean on the car.

"I've got a license for that gun," I said.

"So I see," he said. The gun barrel still pressed under my left ear. "Got a private cop license too. Stay right where you are." He backed two steps to the cruiser and, reaching through the window, honked the horn twice. The Magnum stared stolidly at my stomach.

A Smithfield cop came to the back steps. "Hey, Paul, ask Mr. Bartlett if he knows this guy," the state cop said. Paul disappeared and returned in a minute with Bartlett. Bartlett said, "He's okay. He's a private detective. I hired him to find Kevin. He's okay. Let him come in."

The state cop put the gun away with a nice neat movement, gave me back my own gun, and nodded me toward the house. I went in.

We were in the kitchen again. Margery Bartlett, her face streaked and teary, Bartlett, Trask, the Smithfield cop, and two men I didn't know.

Margery Bartlett said, "Kevin's been kidnapped."

Her husband said, "We got a ransom note today."

One of the men I didn't know said, "I'm Earl Maguire, Spenser," and put out his hand. "I'm Rog's attorney. And this is Lieutenant Healy of the State Police. I think you know Chief Trask." I nodded.

Maguire was small. His grip was hard when he took my hand, and he shook it vigorously. He was dark-skinned with longish black hair carefully layered with a razor cut. Six bucks easy, I thought, for that kind of haircut. I bet the barber wore a black silk coat. He was wearing a form-fitting pale blue denim suit with black stitching along the lapels, blunt-toed, thick-soled black shoes with two-inch heels, a black shirt, and a pale blue figured tie. It must have been his T-Bird outside. BC Law School. Not Harvard, maybe BU, but most likely BC.

"Where'd you go to school?" I said.

"BC," he said. "Why?"

Ah, Spenser, you can do it all, kid. "No reason," I said. "Just wondered."

Healy I knew of. He was chief investigator for the Essex County DA's office. There were at least two first-run racketeers I knew who stayed out of Essex County because they didn't want any truck with him.

Healy said, "Didn't you work for the Suffolk County DA once?"

I said, "Yes."

"Didn't they fire you for hotdogging?"

"I like to call it inner-directed behavior," I said.

"I'll bet you do," Healy said.

He was a medium tall man, maybe five ten, slim, with very square shoulders. His gray hair was cut in a close crew cut, the sideburns trimmed at the top of the ears. The skin on his face looked tight, finely veined on the cheekbones, and his close-shaved cheeks had the faint bluish tinge of heavy beard. He had on a tan seersucker suit and a white shirt and a brown and yellow striped tie. A short-crowned, snap-brimmed straw hat with a flowery hatband lay on the table before him. His hands were folded perfectly still in his lap as he sat with his chair tilted back slightly. He wore a plain gold wedding ring on his left hand.

"What's hotdogging?" Marge Bartlett said.

"He's not too good about regulations," Healy answered.

Margery Bartlett said, "Can you get my child back, Mr. Spenser?" She was leaning forward, biting down on her lower lip with her upper teeth. Her eyes were wide and fixed on me. Her right hand was open on her breast, approximately above her heart. There were tears on her cheeks. Donna Reed in *Ransom*, MGM, 1956. "I don't care about the money; I just want my baby back."

Trask leaned over and patted her hand.

"Don't worry, Marge, we'll get him back for you. You got my word on it." John Wayne, *The Searchers*, Warner Bros. 1956.

I looked at Healy. He was carefully examining the backs of his hands, his lips pursed, whistling silently to himself. The Smithfield cop named Paul was looking closely at the copper switchplate on the wall by the back door.

"What have you got?" I asked Healy.

He handed me a sheet of paper inside a transparent plastic folder. It was a ransom note in the form of a comic strip. The figures were hand-drawn with a red ballpoint pen and showed some skill, like competent graffiti, say. They featured a voluptuous woman in a miniskirt seated on a barstool, leaning on the bar, speaking in voice balloons. "We have your son," she said in the first panel, "and if you don't give us $50,000 you'll never see him again." In the second panel she was taking a drink and saying nothing. In the third panel she said, "Follow the instructions on the next page exactly or it's all over." In the next panel she was lighting a cigarette. In the fifth panel she was full face to the reader and saying, "Be careful." In the sixth and last panel she had turned back to the bar and only her back was visible. I handed it back to Healy. He gave me the second page, similarly enclosed in clear plastic. It was typewritten, single-spaced, by someone who was inexpert at typing.

"Why the hell did they draw the picture?" Roger Bartlett said. "Why did they have to draw pictures? That don't make any sense."

"Take it easy, Rog," Earl Maguire said.

I started to read the typewritten sheet.

"Way to conceal their identity," said Trask. "That's why they're drawing pictures. Right, Healy?"

"Too early to say," Healy said.

It was hot and moist in the kitchen. Outside, the rain had started again. I read the instructions.

> there is a riding stable on route I. In front of it is a driveway. Have Margery Bartlett stand on the curb at the right hand corner of the driveway at High Noon, Sept. 10. Have the money in a green book bag. Have her hold it out in front of her. Have her do that till someone comes along and takes it. If anyone is around or any cops at all or anything goes wrong and you try some funny stuff. Then your kid gets the ax and we mean it. we will cut off his head and send it to you so Don't screw up. AFter we get the money we will tell you where to go and get your kid. So. do what we say and stand by for further instructions.

I gave the paper back to Healy and raised my eyebrows. "Yeah," Healy said. "I know."

"Know what? What do you mean by that?" Marge Bartlett said.

"It's an odd note and an odd set of instructions," I said. "Can you get the fifty?"

Bartlett nodded. "Murray Raymond, down the bank, will gimme the dough. I can put the business up as collateral. I already talked to him, and he's getting me the money from Boston."

"What's funny about the instructions?" Marge Bartlett said. "Why do I have to be there?"

Healy answered her. "I don't know why you have to be there except what they said, maybe to keep some kid from finding the bag and taking it home. The instructions are complicated in the wrong ways. For instance, they obviously want the bag to be where they can grab it on the move, but why there? And why no instructions about the kinds of money and the denominations of the bills? Why give us two days lead time like that to set up a stake?"

"But they needed to give Rog time to get the money," Trask said.

"Yeah, but they didn't need to tell us where they were going to pick it up," I said.

"Right," Healy said. "A call five minutes beforehand would have done that, and left us nothing to do but sit around and wonder."

"And why the mail?" I said.

"What's wrong with the mail?" Roger Bartlett said.

"That's one reason they had to give you lead time," Healy said. "They can't be sure when you'll get the letter, so they have to give themselves away several days ahead."

"What do you mean a stake?" Marge Bartlett asked.

"That's the stakeout," Trask answered. "We conceal ourselves in the adjacent area so's to be in a position to apprehend the kidnappers when they come for the ransom."

"Apprehend," Healy said, and whistled admiringly.

I said, "Adjacent isn't bad either, Lieutenant."

"What's wrong with you guys?" Trask said.

"You talk terrific," I said, "but I'm not sure you want to apprehend the culprits in the adjacent area. Maybe you might want to place them under close surveillance until they lead you to the victim. You know?"

"I don't want anything like that," Margery Bartlett said. And she shook her head. "I want nothing like that at all. They might get mad if they saw you. And they said—about his head—I couldn't stand that."

"I don't want that either," Roger Bartlett said. "I mean, it's only money, you know. I want to do what they say, and when it's over then you can catch them. I mean, it's only money, you know?"

Trask put his hand on Margery Bartlett's again. "We'll do just as you ask, Marge, just as you ask."

Healy shook his head. "A mistake," he said. "Your odds are better on getting the kid back if you let us in on it."

Margery Bartlett looked at me. "What does he mean?"

I took a deep breath. "He means that your best chance to get Kevin back okay is to have us find him. He means they might take the ransom and kill him anyway, or they might not. There's no way to tell. The statistics are slightly in favor of the cops. More kidnap victims survive the kidnapping when rescued by the police than when turned loose by the kidnappers. Not many more; I'd say it's about fifty-five percent to forty-five percent."

Healy said, "Maybe a little closer. But what else have you got?"

Roger Bartlett said, "I don't want him hurt."

Margery Bartlett put her face down in her hands and began to wail.

Her husband put one arm around her shoulder. She

shrugged it away and cried louder. "Marge," he said. "Jesus, Marge, we gotta do something. Spenser, what should we do?" Tears formed in his eyes and began to slide down his face.

I said, "We'll stake it out."

"But . . ."

"We'll stake it out," I said again. "We'll be cool about it. We got two days to set it up."

Trask said, "Now just hold on, Spenser. This is my town, and I decide whether or not we do any surveillance."

Healy let the front legs of his chair down slowly to the floor, put his folded hands on the tabletop, leaned forward slightly, and with no inflection in his voice said, "George, please keep your trap shut until we are finished talking." Trask flushed. He opened his mouth and closed it. He looked hard at Healy for a minute, and then his eyes shifted away.

"Now," Healy continued. "George, here's what I want you to do. I want you to go down to the town hall and get some maps of that area from the surveyor's office and bring them back. And together we will go over them." He turned toward the Smithfield patrolman named Paul. "Marsh, I want you to take these two items into Ten-ten Commonwealth and have the crime lab go over them. You know people in there?"

Paul said, "Yessir, I been in there before."

Healy handed him the two envelopes. Paul started to leave, looked uncertainly at Trask, then at Healy. Healy nodded. Paul left, holding the two envelopes under his raincoat. Trask sat looking at his knuckles. The muscles at his jaw hinge were clenched. There was a tic in his left eyelid.

"The maps, George," Healy said. Their eyes locked again, briefly. Then Trask got up, put on a yellow slicker, and went out. He slammed the door. In the kitchen it was quiet except for Margery Bartlett's sobbing. Her husband stood about three feet from her, his arms hanging straight down as if he didn't know what to do with them.

Earl Maguire said, "We'd better get a doctor over here. He can give her something. Who's your doctor, Rog? I'll call him for you."

"It's there by the phone," Bartlett said. "Croft, Doctor Croft. Have him come over. Tell him what happened. Tell him she needs something. That's a good idea. Tell him to come over and give her something."

Healy stood up, took off his coat, hung it over the back of his chair, loosened his tie, and sat back down. He nodded toward the chair Trask had left. "Sit down, Spenser," he said. "We got some work to do."

5

Margery Bartlett had gone upstairs to lie down, Dr. Croft had come over and given her a shot. Roger Bartlett had gone to a neighbor's house to pick up his daughter. Trask had brought back the maps, and he and Healy and I were looking at them spread out on the kitchen table. A small slick-haired state cop in plainclothes and rimless glasses had hooked a tape recorder to the phone in the den off the kitchen and sat next to it with earphones, reading a copy of *Playboy* he'd found in the magazine rack. He turned it sideways to look at the centerfold.

"Sonova bitch," he said, "hair and all. You see this, Lieutenant?"

Healy didn't look up. "If you gotta read that garbage, read it, but don't narrate it."

The little cop held the magazine out at arm's length. "Sonova bitch," he said.

Healy said, "What's up here, back of the riding stable?"

"Nothing," Trask said, "just woods. It's the west end of the Lynn Woods. Runs for miles back on into Lynn."

"Hills?"

"Yeah, low ones; it slopes up back of the stable riding ring."

"Can we put someone up there with glasses?"

"Sure, the woods are thick. He could climb a tree if he wanted."

"You know the people at the stable?"

"Sure."

"Can we put somebody in there?"

"In the stable?"

Healy said, "I don't mean inside the stable. Can we have someone posing as an employee?"

"Oh yeah, sure. I'll set it up."

Healy made some notes on a small notepad he'd taken from inside his coat. He used a big red fountain pen that looked like one my father had used when I was small.

"If they pick up the money here," I said, "that's northbound. Where's the first place they can get onto Route 1 north?"

"Saugus," Healy said. "Here, by the shopping center."

"And the first place they can get off?"

"Here, about two hundred yards up, at this intersection. Otherwise they could dip down through the underpass here and head up Route 1 or turn off here at 128. We can put a couple of people at each place."

"And a walkie-talkie up on the hill with the glasses?"

Healy nodded. "We'll put an unmarked car here." He put a cross on the map at the intersection of Route 1 and Salem Street. "Here, here, he could U-turn at the lights. So here, southbound." Healy marked out eleven positions on the map.

"That's a lot of cars," Trask said.

"I know. We'll put your people use their own cars and supply them with walkie-talkies. How many people can you give me?"

"Everybody; twelve men. But who's going to pay them per diem?"

Healy looked at him. "Per diem?"

"For the cars. They're supposed to get a per diem

mileage allowance for the use of their own cars on official business. This could mount up if all of them do it. And I have to answer to a town meeting every year."

I said, "Do you accept Master Charge?"

Trask said, "It's not funny. You've never had to answer to a town meeting. They're a bunch of unreasonable bastards at those things."

Healy said, "The state will rent the cars. I'll sign a voucher. But if you screw this up, you'll learn what an unreasonable bastard really is."

"There won't be any screw-up. I'll be right on top of every move my people make."

"Yeah," Healy said.

"Who you going to put into the stable?" I asked Healy.

"You want to do it? You're the least likely to be recognized."

"Yeah."

"You know anything about horses?"

"Only what I read in the green sheet."

"It doesn't matter. We'll go up and look around."

Healy put on his coat, tightened his tie, put the snap-brimmed straw hat squarely on his head, and we went out. The rain had started again. Healy ignored it. "We'll go in your car," he said. "No need to have them looking at the radio car parked up there. Stick here, Miles," he said to the cop leaning against the cruiser. He had on a yellow rain slicker now. "I'll be back."

"Yes, sir," Miles said.

I backed out, pulling the car up on the grass to get around the state cruiser.

"Your roof leaks," Healy said.

"Maybe I can get the state to give me per diem payment for a new one," I said.

Healy said nothing. The stable was about ten minutes

from the Bartletts' home. We drove there in silence. I pulled
into the parking lot in front of the stable, parked, and shut
off the motor. The stable was maybe one hundred yards in
from the road. The access to it was between a restaurant and
a liquor store. The restaurant was roadside colonial: brick,
dark wood and white plastic, flat-roofed. In front was an
enormous incongruous red and yellow sign that advertised
home cooking and family-style dining and cocktails. The
store was glass-fronted; the rest was artificial fieldstone. It
too had a flat roof rimmed in white plastic. In the window
was an inflated panda with a sign around his neck
advertising a summer cooler. Across the top of the store was
a sign that said Package Store in pink neon. Two of the
letters were out. The parking lot narrowed to a driveway
near the stable.

The stable looked like someplace you'd go to rent a
donkey. It was a one-story building with faded maroon
siding, the kind that goes on in four-by-eight pregrooved
panels. The trim was white, and the nails had bled through
so that it was rust streaked. The roof was shingled partly in
red and partly in black. Through it poked three tin
chimneys. Next to it was a riding ring of unpainted boards
and the trailer part of a tractor trailer rig, rusted and tireless
on cinder blocks. In front of the stable parked among the
weeds were five horse trailers, an old green dump truck with
V-8 on the front, an aqua-colored '65 Chevy hardtop, a new
Cadillac convertible, and a tan '62 Chevy wagon. A sign,
Solid Fill Wanted, stood at the edge of the road, and a pile
of old asphalt, bricks, paving stones, tree stumps, gravel,
crushed stone, sewer pipe, a rusting hot water tank, three
railroad ties, and a bicycle frame settled into the marshy
ground behind it. Marlboro country.

Healy looked at it all without speaking. Carefully. A sea
gull lit on the containerized garbage back of the restaurant

and began working on a chunk of something I couldn't identify through the rain.

"Let's get out," Healy said. We did. The rain was steady and warm and vertical. No wind slanted it. Healy had on no raincoat but seemed not to notice. I turned the collar up on my raincoat. We walked down toward the stable. The bare earth around it had been softened into a swamp of mud, and it became hard to walk. On the other side of the riding ring a handmade sign said Bridle Path, and an arrow pointed to a narrow trail that led into the woods. We walked back out to the parking lot and stood at the edge of Route 1 at the spot where Mrs. Bartlett was to stand. Cars rushed past in a hiss of wet pavement. To the left the road curved out of sight beyond a hill. To the right it dipped into a tunnel with a service road branching off to the right and parallel. Two hundred yards down was a light on the service road and a cross street.

Healy turned and headed back toward the stable. I followed. Healy seemed to assume I would. I walked a little faster so I'd be beside him, not behind him. I was beginning to feel like a trainee.

At the far end of the stable was a door marked Office. The torn screen door was shut, but the wooden door inside was open and a television set was tuned to a talk show. "Were you first into transcendental meditation before or after you made this picture?" "During, actually. We were in location in Spain . . ." Healy rapped on the door, and a dark-haired man answered. He was wearing black Levi's jeans and a white T-shirt that was too small for him. His stomach spilled over his belt and showed bare where the T-shirt gapped. His skin was dark and moist-looking, and his face sank into several layers of carelessly shaved chin. He went perfectly with the stable. He also smelled strongly of garlic and beer.

"Yeah?"

I said, "I'd like to rent a high-spirited palomino stallion with a hand-tooled Spanish leather saddle and silver-studded bridle, please." The man looked at me with his eyes squinting, as if the light were too bright.

"A what?" he said.

"Shut up, Spenser," Healy said and showed his badge to the fat man. "May we come in, please?"

The fat man stepped back from the door. "Sure, sure, come on in; I'm just having lunch."

We went in. The television was on top of a rolltop desk. The actress was saying to the talk show hostess, "Sylvia, I never pay any attention to the critics." On the writing surface of the desk were a big wedge of cheese and a salami on the white butcher's paper in which they'd been wrapped. There was also a half-empty quart bottle of Pickwick ale, an open pocketknife, and a jar of pickled sweet peppers. The fat man belched as he waved us to a seat. Or waved Healy to a seat. There was only a straight-backed chair by the desk and a sprung swivel chair with a torn cushion on it. The fat man sat in the swivel chair, Healy took the straight chair, and I stood. "The critics I care about, Sylvia, are those people out there. If I can make them happy, I feel that I'm . . ." Healy reached over and shut off the television.

"What's up?" the fat man said.

"My name is Healy. I'm a detective lieutenant with the Massachusetts State Police. I want to have this man spend the next two days here as if he were an employee, and I don't want to tell you why."

A dirty white cat jumped up on the desk and began to chew on a scrap of salami. The fat man ignored it and cut a piece of cheese off the wedge. He speared it with the jackknife and popped it into his mouth. With the other hand he fished a pickled pepper out of the jar and ate it. Then he drank most of the rest of the ale from the bottle, belched again, and said, "Well, for crissake, Lieutenant, I got a right to know what's happening. I mean, for crying out loud, I don't want to screw up my business, you know. I got a right."

Healy said, "You gotta right to discuss with the building inspector the code violations he and I are going to spot in this manure bin if you give me any trouble."

The fat man blinked a minute at Healy and then said, "Yeah, sure, okay. Look, always glad to help out. I was just curious, you know. I don't want no trouble. Be glad to have this fellow around."

Healy said, "Thank you. He'll be here tomorrow morning dressed for work, and he'll hang around here for the next couple of days. I don't want you to say anything about this to anyone. It is a matter of life and death, and if anyone starts talking about this, it could be fatal. Kind of fatal for you too. Got me?"

"You can trust me, Lieutenant. I won't say nothing to nobody. Don't worry about it." He looked at me. "You're welcome to stay around all you want. My name's Vinnie. What's yours?"

"Nick Charles," I said. He grabbed my hand.

"Good to meet you, Nick. Anything you need, just holler. Want a piece of cheese or salami, anything?"

"No, thanks." Vinnie looked at Healy. Healy shook his head.

"Remember, Vinnie, keep your mouth shut about this. It matters."

"Right, Lieutenant. Mum's the word. Wild horses . . ."

"Yeah, okay. Just remember." Healy left. I followed.

6

I spent two days hanging around the riding stable and learned only that horses are not smart. Vinnie spent most of his time in with the TV and the Pickwick. And assorted kids, more girls than boys, in scraggly Levi's jeans and scuffed riding boots and white T-shirts which hung outside the jeans fed the horses and exercised them in the oozy ring and occasionally rented one to someone, usually a kid, who would ride it off into the bridle trail. I looked good in a plaid shirt with the sleeves cut off and a pair of jeans and high-laced tan work shoes. I had a gun stuck in the waistband under the shirt, and it dug into my stomach all day. For a prop I had a big wooden rake, and I spent the days moving horse manure around with it while I whistled "Home on the Range."

Pickup day was beautiful, eighty-two degrees, mild breeze, cloudless sunshine. A day for looking at a ball game or walking along with a girl and a jug of apple wine or casting for a smallmouth black bass where an elm tree hung out over the Ipswich River. That kind of a day. A day for collecting ransom, I supposed, if that was your style. I straightened up and stretched and looked around. Healy should have everyone in place by now. I saw nothing. The hill behind the stable culminated in a water tower; up in a

57

tree near it there was supposed to be a guy with glasses and a walkie-talkie. I looked for sun flash on the lenses. I didn't see any. Healy would see that there was no lens flash. Just as he'd see that the two guys in Palm Beach suits he had in the window booth of the restaurant wouldn't be oiling their blackjacks. I looked at my watch—quarter to twelve. Marge Bartlett was supposed to arrive at noon. High noon the letter had said. I wondered if there was a low noon. No one would make an appointment for it if there was.

I went back to the manure. In the woods behind the riding ring cicadas droned steadily in pleasnt monotony. Now and then in the stable a horse would snort, or rattle a hoof against the stall. Several sea gulls were doing a good business in the garbage container back of the restaurant. I checked the parking lot again out of the corner of my eye. Marge Bartlett was there. Just getting out of her red Mustang. She went to the edge of the driveway carrying the green canvas book bag full of money and stood. She was dressed for a bullfight. Tight gold toreador pants with a row of buttons along the wide flare. A ruffled red shirt, a bronze-colored leather vest that reached to her thighs and closed with two big leather thongs across the stomach, high-heeled bronze boots with lacings, a bronze wide-brimmed vaquero hat, bronze leather gloves. I'd always wondered what to wear to a ransom payment. Traffic went by. Usually cars, now and then a truck downshifting as it came up the hill beyond the curve. Occasionally a motorcycle loud and whining. Noisy bastards. My hands were sweaty on the rake handle. My neck and shoulder muscles felt tight. I kept shrugging my shoulders, but they didn't loosen. I stood the rake against the stable and went and sat on a bale of straw against the wall. I'd brought lunch in a paper bag so I could be sitting and eating and looking when the pickup was made. A big refrigerator truck lumbered by on the highway. Marge Bartlett stood rigid and still, looking straight ahead with the bag held at her side. The sea gulls rustled away at the garbage. Somewhere in the woods a dog barked. Down the highway another motorcycle snarled. It appeared around the curve. A big one, three-fifty probably, high-rise handlebars, rearview mirror, small front wheel, sissy bar behind. My favorite kind. It swung into the parking lot, and without stopping the rider took the bag from Marge Bartlett, took one turn around the mirror support with the straps, and headed straight across the parking lot toward the stable.

Bridle path, I thought as he went by me. The license plates were covered. I got one flash of Levi's jeans and engineer's boots and field jacket and red plastic helmet with blue plastic face shield, and he was behind the riding ring into the bridle path and gone in the woods. I could hear the roar of the bike dwindle, and then I couldn't hear it, and all there was was the drone of the cicadas. And the traffic. Bridle path. Sonova bitch. A lot of per diem shot to hell.

Marge Bartlett got back in her Mustang and drove away. I threw my sandwich at the sea gulls, and they flared up and then came down on it and tore it apart. I stood up and took the rake from against the wall and broke the handle across my knee and dropped the two parts on the ground and started for my car. Then I stopped and took a ten-dollar bill out of my wallet and went back and folded it around one of the rake tines and left it there. Vinnie didn't look as if he could afford my temper tantrum. With the profits he'd shown in the two days I'd spent there, he couldn't buy a pocket comb.

Healy and Trask were sitting in the front seat of Trask's cruiser in the parking lot of the Catholic church four blocks from the stable. There was a map spread out against the dashboard in front of them. I pulled up beside them and shut off the engine.

"Your man in the tree spot them?" I asked.

"Nope, lost him as soon as he went into the woods. The trees overhang the trail."

Trask said, "The goddamned trail splits and runs off in all different directions. There's no real way to tell where it comes out. Some of the people riding have made new trails. He could have come out in Lynn, in Saugus, in Smithfield past the roadblock. He's gone."

Healy's face was stiff and the bones showed. He said, "Two days, two goddamned days looking at that place, looking at that goddamned bridle path sign, listening to motorcycles going by on Route 1. Two days. And we stood there with our thumb in our butt. For crissake, Spenser, you were there, you saw people riding into that path; why the hell didn't you put it together? You're supposed to be a goddamned hotshot."

"I'm not a big intellect like you state dicks. I was overextended raking the manure."

Healy took the map of the woods he'd been looking at and began to wad it into a ball, packing it in his thin freckled hands the way we used to make snowballs when I was a kid. The radio in Trask's car crackled, and the dispatcher said something I couldn't understand. Trask responded.

"This is Trask."

Again the radio in its crackly mechanical voice. And Trask. "Roger, out." Jiminy, just like in the movies. "Aren't you supposed to say 'Ten Four'?" I said.

Trask turned his big red face at me. "Look, you screwed this thing up, and you feel like a horse's ass now. Don't take it out on me." He looked at Healy. "Did you get that on the radio?" Healy nodded. I said, "What was it?"

"The Bartletts got a phone call from the kidnappers telling them where to get the kid." He put the car in gear and backed out of the parking lot. I followed. Maybe they'll give him back, I thought. Maybe.

7

The call had come perhaps ten minutes after the money had been picked up. The little slick-haired cop had recorded it, and he played it back for Trask and Healy and me. Roger Bartlett said, "Hello." There was a brief scrap of music and a voice said, "Howdy all you kidnapping freaks," in the affected southern drawl that is required of everyone who is under thirty and cool. "This is your old buddy the kidnapper speaking, and we gotta big treat for you all out there in kidnap land. The big prizewinners in our pay-the-ransom contest are Mr. and Mrs. Roger Bartlett of Smithfield." The music came up again and then faded, and several male voices sang a jingle:

> Behind a school in old Smithfield
> First prize your ransom it did yield,
> So in that direction you should be steering,
> From us no longer you'll be hearing.

Then the music came up and faded out with some giggles behind it. Roger Bartlett said to us, "He's gotta be behind one of the schools. There's six: the four elementary, the junior high, the high school . . ." Trask said, "What about Our Lady's?" And Bartlett said, "Right, the Catholic

62

school," and Healy said, "How about kindergartens? How many private kindergartens in town?"

Trask looked at Bartlett; Bartlett shook his head. Trask shrugged and said, "Hell, I don't know."

Healy said, "Okay, Trask, run it down; get your people checking behind and around all the schools in town. And don't miss anything like a dog school or a driving school. These are odd people."

Trask went out to his car and got on the radio. Bartlett went with him. I said to Healy, "What in Christ have we got here?"

Healy shook his head. "I don't know. I don't remember anything like this anywhere. Do you realize the trouble they went to, to rig up that tape recording?"

"Yeah," I said, "and it's not just to conceal voices. There's something else going on. Something personal in this thing. The ransom note, this call—there's something wrong."

Margery Bartlett came in with Earl Maguire. "What's wrong?" she said. "Is something wrong? Have you found Kevin?"

"Nothing's wrong, ma'am," Healy said. "Spenser was talking about something else. Chief Trask is directing the search for Kevin now. I'm sure there will be good news soon."

But Healy didn't believe it and I knew he didn't and he knew I knew. He looked very steadily at me after he'd said it. I looked away. Maguire said, "Sit down, Marge, no sense tiring yourself." She sat at the kitchen table. Maguire sat opposite her. Healy looked out the back door at Trask. I leaned against the counter. The big Lab that I'd seen my first visit wandered into the kitchen and lapped water noisily from his dish.

Marge Bartlett said, "Punkin, you naughty dog, don't be

so noisy." Punkin? The dog was big enough to pull a beer wagon. He stopped drinking and flopped down on his side in the middle of the floor. No one said anything. The dog heaved a big sigh, and his stomach rolled.

Marge Bartlett said again, "Punkin! You should be ashamed." He paid her no attention. "I apologize for my dog," she said. "But dogs are good. They don't demand much of you; they just love you for what you are. Just accept you. I'm doing a sculpture of Punkin in clay. I want to capture that trusting and undemanding quality."

I saw Healy's shoulders straighten, heard Trask's car door slam, and Trask pushed into the kitchen with Roger Bartlett.

Trask said to Healy, "Junior high school, come on." Healy went. I went after them. Trask already had the car in gear as I jumped into the backseat. He spun gravel out of the driveway, and the siren was whoop-whooping by the time he was in third gear.

It was maybe three minutes to the junior high school. Trask wrenched the cruiser into the big semicircular driveway in front of it with a screech of rubber and brakes and spun off that and onto the hot-top parking surface to the left of the school and on around behind it. He loved the noise and the siren. I bet he'd been dying to do that since the case began. There were maybe two dozen cars parked against the back of the two-story brick building. Most of them were small cars, suitable for junior high school teachers. On the end of the second row of cars was an old Cadillac hearse. The back door was open, and a group of kids stood around it, held back by two prowl car cops in short sleeves and sunglasses. The patrol car, blue light still turning, was parked beside the hearse. In the school windows most of the other kids were leaning out and some were yelling. The teachers were not having much luck with them. Most weren't trying but craned out the windows with the kids.

Trask jammed on the brakes and was out of the car while it was still lurching. He left the door open behind him and strode to the hearse. Healy got out, closed his door, and followed. I sat in the backseat a minute and looked at the hearse. I felt a little sick. I didn't want to look inside. I wanted to go home. There was a case of Amstel beer home in the refrigerator. I wanted to go home and drink it. I got out of the car and followed Healy.

Inside the hearse was a coffin made of scrap plywood. The plywood wasn't new, and the carpentry was not professional. It was padlocked. One of the prowl car cops got a tire iron, and Trask, squatting in the hearse, pried the hasp off. Healy lifted the lid. I bit down hard on my back teeth. A life-sized rag doll dummy sat bolt upright in the coffin and leered at us with its red Raggedy Andy lips. Still squatting, Trask started back with a yelp, lost his balance, and sat down awkwardly on the floor of the hearse. Healy never moved. The dummy flopped over sideways, and I could see a rusty spring attached to its back. I realized that my right hand was on the gun butt under my shirt. I took it away and rubbed it on my pants leg. The crowd was absolutely still. I said, "Trick or treat."

Healy said, "Get that thing out of there."

The two patrolmen lifted it out of the hearse and set it on the ground. Healy and I squatted down beside it.

"Shirt and pants stuffed with newspaper," Healy said. "Head seems to be made out of a pillowcase stuffed with cotton batting. Features drawn on with Magic Marker. Spring looks like it came from an easy chair."

He stood up. "Trask," he said, "keep people away from this area. I'll have some technicians come down and assist your people on the fingerprints and all."

Trask nodded. "Okay," he snapped to the crowd, "back it up. We've got to get lab specialists right on this." He spoke to the two prowlies. "Move 'em back, men. We'll seal this area off."

I wondered if he rode a white stallion in the Memorial Day parade.

Behind the school was an athletic field ringed with high evergreen woods. Healy walked out toward the trees; I walked along with him. He paused on the pitcher's mound and picked up some clay and rolled it in his right hand. He looked down at the pitching rubber. And then at home plate. He took his hat off and wiped his forearm across his forehead. He put his hat back on tipped low forward, shading his eyes, and looked out toward center field and the trees beyond it. He put his hands in his back pockets and rocked silently on the mound, his back toward home plate, staring out at the trees behind center field.

"Ever play ball, Spenser?"

"Some."

"I was a pitcher. All-State at Winthrop High School. Had a tryout with the Phillies. Coulda signed but the war was on. When I got out of the army, I was married, had two kids already. Had to get a steady job. Went with the state cops instead."

I didn't say anything. Healy continued to look at center field, his head tipped back a little to see out under the brim of his hat.

"Almost thirty years."

I didn't answer. He wasn't really talking to me, anyway.

"Got any kids, Spenser?"

"Nope."

"I got five. The little one is fifteen now; only one left at home. Plays for St. John's. He's a pitcher."

Healy stopped talking. The wind moved the pine

branches in the woods. The trees had a strong smell in the September heat. Some starlings hopped about the infield near second base, pecking at the grass. Behind us the police radio squawked.

"Sonova goddamned bitch!" he said.

I nodded. "Me too," I said.

8

State and local cops swarmed over the hearse like ants on a marshmallow and learned nothing. It had been stolen six months before from two brothers in Revere who had bought it at a sheriff's sale and were going to fix it up as a camper. There were no fingerprints which meant anything to anyone. There was no opium stashed in the spare tire well, no hardcore porn taped to the chassis, no automatic weapons being smuggled to the counterculture. There were no laundry marks in the shirt and pants. The newspapers used to stuff the dummy were recent issues of *The Boston Globe* obtainable at any newsstand. The plywood and the hardware from which the coffin had been made were standard and could have come from any lumberyard in the country. There were no lube stickers or antifreeze tags anywhere on the vehicle to tell us anything. In short, the hearse was as blank and meaningless as a Styrofoam coffee cup.

Marge Bartlett was under sedation again. Roger Bartlett was mad, scared, and mournful. It was the mad that showed. As I left he was yelling at Healy and at Trask. He'd already yelled at me.

"Goddamn it! What's going on? You people have found nothing. What's going on? Where's my son? I did what you said, and I get the bullshit with the funny coffin. You people have found nothing . . ." The door closed behind me. I didn't blame him for yelling. I looked at my watch—four fifteen. Time to go home.

When I got home the Amstel beer was still there in the refrigerator, a gift from a girl who knew the way to my heart. I popped the cap off a bottle and drank half of it. Jesus, the Dutch knew how to live. I remembered a café in a hotel in Amsterdam where Amstel was the house beer. I finished the beer, opened another, drank some while I got undressed, put it on the sink while I took a shower, finished it while I toweled off.

I went to the kitchen in my shorts, opened a third bottle, picked up the phone, and called information. I got Susan Silverman's number and called her. Her voice sounded very educated on the phone. She said, "Hello."

I said, "Help."

She said, "I beg your pardon?"

I said, "I am in desperate need of guidance. Do you make house calls?"

She said, "Who is this?"

I said, "How quickly they forget. Spenser. You remember . . . proud carriage, clear blue eyes that never waver, intrepid chin, white raincoat that makes me look taller?"

And she said, "Oh, that Spenser."

"I know it's late," I said, "but I'm about to cook a pork tenderloin *en croûte* and wondered if you would be willing to eat some of it while we talk more about Kevin Bartlett." She was silent. "I'm a hell of a cook," I said. "Not much of a detective, have some trouble locating my own Adam's apple, don't have much success with kidnapping victims, but I'm a hell of a cook."

"Mr. Spenser, it's five thirty. I was just about to put my own supper in the oven."

"I'll come out and get you if you wish," I said. "If you'd rather, I'll buy you dinner."

"No," she said. I could almost hear her make up her mind. "I'll come in. What is your address?"

"Do you know where Marlborough Street is?" I asked.

"Yes."

"Okay, I'm in the last block before you get to the Public Garden." I gave her the number. "It's on the left-hand side. How long will it take you?"

"Would seven thirty be all right?"

"Just right," I said. "I'll look for you then."

She said good-bye and we hung up. "Ha!" I said out loud. I drank down the rest of my beer to celebrate. Still got the old sex appeal, kid, still got all the old moves. She couldn't resist me. Or maybe she just liked pork tenderloin *en croûte*.

I turned on the oven to preheat, took the pork out of the meatkeeper to warm up, and set about making the crust. I opened another Amstel. Better watch it, though; didn't want to be drunk when she got here. It was, after all, business, or partly business. I made a very short crust and laid the tenderloin across it. I sprinkled in some thyme, some black pepper, and a dust of dill. I rolled the crust carefully around it and put it on a roasting pan. I brushed a little egg white on the top to glaze it and put it in a medium oven.

I peeled and sliced three green apples, some carrots, and some red onions. I added a lump of butter and put them to simmer in about an inch of cider in a tightly covered sauce pan. I made a Cumberland sauce for the pork. Then I went to get dressed. I decided against a gold lamé smoking jacket and white silk scarf. Instead I put on a black polo shirt and white trousers with a modest flare. I put on my black loafers, still shined, and walked up Arlington Street two blocks to Boylston and bought two loaves of hot French bread from a bake shop. Then I walked back to my apartment and put a bottle of red wine in the wine bucket, opened it to let it breathe, and packed it in ice. I knew that was bad—I was supposed to roll it on my palate at room temperature, but once a hick, always a hick, I guess. I liked it cold.

9

At seven fifteen I took the pork out of the oven and put it on the counter to rest. I took the lid off the vegetables, turned up the heat, and boiled away the moisture while I shook the pan gently. It made them glaze slightly. I put them in a covered chafing dish over a low blue flame. I put the French bread into the still warm oven. I had stopped on the way back from Smithfield and bought a dozen native tomatoes at a farm stand. Each was the size of a softball. I sliced two of them about a half-inch thick and sprinkled them lightly with sugar and arranged them slightly overlapping on a bed of Boston lettuce on a platter and put them beside the roast to warm up. Tomatoes are much better at room temperature.

I had just finished washing my hands and face when the doorbell rang. Everything was ready. Ah, Spenser, what a touch. Everything was just right except that I couldn't seem to find a missing child. Well, nobody's perfect. I pushed the release button and opened my apartment door. I was wrong. Susan Silverman was perfect.

It took nearly forty years of savoir faire to keep from saying "Golly." She had on black pants and a knit yellow scoop-necked, short-sleeved sweater that gaped fractionally above the black pants, showing a fine and only occasional line of tan skin. The sleeves were short and had a scalloped frill, and her black and yellow platform shoes made her damned near my height. Her black and yellow earrings were cubed pendants. Her black hair glistened, her teeth were bright in her tan face when she smiled and put out her hand.

"Come in," I said. Very smooth. I didn't scuff my foot; I didn't mumble. I stood right up straight when I said it. I don't think I blushed.

"This is a very nice apartment," she said as she stepped into the living room. I said thank you. She walked across and looked at the wood carving on the server. "Isn't this the statue of the Indian in front of the museum?"

"Yes."

"It's lovely. Where did you get it?"

This time I think I did blush. "Aw hell," I said.

"Did you do it?"

"Yes."

"Oh, it's very good." She ran her hands over the wood. "What kind of wood is it?"

"Hard pine," I said.

"How did you get the wood so smooth?"

"I rubbed it down with powdered pumice and a little mineral oil."

"It is very lovely," she said. "Did you do all these wood carvings?" I nodded. She looked at me and shook her head. "And you cook too?"

I nodded again.

"Amazing," she said.

"Can I get you a drink?" I said.

"I'd love one."

"Would you take a vodka gimlet?"

"That would be splendid," she said. Splendid. In her mouth it sounded just right. Anyone else who said "splendid" would have sounded like the wrong end of a horse.

I put five parts of vodka and one part Rose's lime juice in

a pitcher, stirred it with ice, and strained some into two short glasses.

"Would you care to sit on a stool and drink it while I make last-minute motions in the kitchen?"

"I'll do better than that, I'll help set the table while I'm drinking my drink."

"Okay."

The kitchen area was separated from the living-dining area by a waist-high partition and some lathe-turned risers extending to the ceiling. As I poured oil and vinegar over the tomatoes, I watched her through the partition. She was probably between thirty-five and forty. Her body was strong, and as she bent over the table placing the silverware her thighs were firm and smooth and her back and waist graceful and resilient where the blouse gapped. She moved surely, and I bet myself she played good tennis.

I sliced half the pork *en croûte* in quarter-inch slices and arranged them on the serving platter. I put the chafing dish of vegetables on the table, put the tomatoes and roast out also. Susan Silverman's glass was empty, and I filled it. My head was feeling a little thick from five beers and a large gimlet. Some would say a thickness of head was my normal condition.

"Candles too hokey?" I said.

She laughed and said, "I think so."

"Shall we finish our drinks before we eat?" I asked.

"If you wish."

She sat at the end of the couch and leaned back slightly against the arm, took a grown-up sip of her gimlet, and looked at me over the glass as she did so.

"What ever happened to your nose, Mr. Spenser?"

"A very good heavyweight boxer hit it several times with his left fist."

"Why didn't you ask him not to do that?"

"It's considered bad form. I was hoping for the referee."

"You don't seem to choose the easiest professions," she said.

"I don't know. The real pain, I think, would be nine to five at a desk processing insurance claims. I'd rather get my nose broken weekly."

Her glass was empty. I filled it from the pitcher and freshened mine. Don't want to get drunk on duty. Don't want to make a damned fool of myself in front of Susan Silverman, either.

She smiled her thanks at me. "So, sticking your nose into things and getting it broken allows you to live life on your own terms, perhaps."

"Jesus, I wish I'd said that," I said. "Want to eat?"

"I think we'd better; I'm beginning to feel the gimlets."

"In that case, my dear, let me get you another." I raised my eyebrows and flicked an imaginary cigar.

"Oh, do the funny walk, Groucho," she said.

"I haven't got that down yet," I said. I gestured toward the pitcher, and she shook her head. "No thank you, really."

I held her chair as she sat down, sat down opposite her, and poured some wine in her glass.

"A self-effacing little domestic red," I said, "with just a hint of presumption."

She took a sip. "Oh, good," she said, "it's cold. I hate it at room temperature, don't you?"

I said, "Let's elope."

"Just like that," she said. "Because I like cold wine?"

"Well, there are other factors," I said.

"Let's eat first," she said.

We ate. Largely in silence. There are people with whom silence is not strained. Very few of them are women. But Susan Silverman was one. She didn't make conversation.

Or if she was making conversation she was so good at it that I didn't notice. She ate with pleasure and impeccable style. Me too.

She accepted another slice of the roast and put sauce on it from the gravy boat.

"The sauce is super," she said. "What is it?"

"Cumberland sauce," I said. "It is also terrific with duck."

She didn't ask for the recipe. Style. I hate people who ask for recipes.

"Well, it is certainly terrific with pork."

"Jesus Christ," I said.

"What's the matter?"

"You're Jewish."

"Yes?"

"You're not Orthodox?"

"No."

"Serving a pork roast on your first date with a Jewish lady is not always considered a slick move."

She laughed. "I didn't even think of that. You poor thing. Of course it is not a slick move. But is this a date? I thought I was going to be questioned."

"Yeah. That's right. I'm just softening you up now. After dessert and brandy I break out the strappado."

She held out her wineglass. "Well then, I'd better fortify myself as best I can."

I poured her more wine.

"What about Kevin Bartlett? Where do you think he is?"

She shrugged. "I don't know. How could I? Haven't you got any clues at all?"

"Oh yeah, we got clues. We got lots of clues. But they don't lead us to anything. What they tell us is that we're into something weird. It's freak-land again."

"Again?"

"That's just nostalgia, I guess. Used to be when you got a kidnapping you assumed the motive to be greed and you could count on that and work with it. You ran into a murder and you could figure lust or profit as a starter. Now you gotta wonder if it's political, religious, or merely idiosyncratic. You know, for the hell of it. Because it's there."

"And you yearn for the simple crimes like Leopold-Loeb?"

"Yeah," I grinned. "Or Ruth Judd, the ax murderess. Okay, so maybe there was always freaky crime. It just seems more prevalent. Or maybe I grow old."

"Maybe we all do," she said.

"Yeah, but I'd like to find Kevin Bartlett before I get senile. You know about the kidnapping note and the hearse and the dummy?"

"Some. The story was all over the school system when they found the hearse behind the junior high. But I don't know details."

"Okay," I said, "here they are." I told her. "Now," I said, and gestured with the wine bottle toward her glass.

"Half a glass," she said. I poured. "That's good."

"Now," I said again, "do you think he was kidnapped? And if he was kidnapped, was it just for money?"

"In order," she said, "I don't know, and no."

"Yeah, that's about where I am," I said. "Tell me about this group he ran with."

"As I said when you saw me the other day in my office, I really know very little about them. I've heard that there is a group of disaffected young people who have formed a commune of some sort. Commune may be too strong a word. There is a group, and I only know this from gossip in the high school, which chooses to live together. I don't want to stereotype them. They are mostly, I've heard, school- and college-age people who do not go to school or work in the traditional sense. I've heard that they have a house somewhere around Smithfield."

"Who owns the house?"

"I don't know, but there is a kind of leader, an older man, maybe thirty or so, this Vic Harroway. I would think he'd be the owner."

"And Kevin was hanging around with this group?"

"With some of them. Or at least with some kids who were said to be associated with this group. I'd see him now and then sitting on the cemetery wall across from the common with several kids from the group. Or *maybe* from the group. I'm making this sound a good deal more positive than it is. I'm not sure of any of this or of even the existence of such a group. Although I'm inclined to think there is a group like that."

"Who would know?"

She frowned. "I don't know. Chief Trask, I suppose."

"How bizarre is this group?"

"Bizarre? I don't know. I hadn't heard anything very bizarre about them. I imagine there's grass smoked there, although not many of us find that bizarre anymore. Other than that I can't think of anything particularly bizarre. What kind of bizarre do you mean?"

The wine was gone, and I was looking a little wistfully at the empty bottle. It was hard concentrating on business. I was also looking a little wistfully at Susan Silverman. Neither rain nor sleet nor snow nor dark of night maybe, but red wine and a handsome woman—that was something else.

She said, "What kind of bizarre are you looking for?"

"Any kind at all. The kind of bizarre that would be capable of that dummy trick in the coffin, the kind of bizarre that would make a singing commercial out of the telephone call. The kind of bizarre that would do the ransom note in a comic strip. Would you like some brandy?"

"One small glass."

"Let's take it to the living room."

She sat where she had before, at one end of the couch. I gave her some Calvados and sat on the coffee table near her.

"I don't know anything bizarre about the group. I have the impression that there is something unusual about Vic Harroway, but I don't know quite what it is."

"Think about it. Who said he was odd? What context was his oddness in?"

She frowned again. "No, just an idea that he's unusual."

"Is he unusual in appearance?"

"I don't know."

"Size?"

"Really, I can't recall."

"Is he unusual in his sex habits?"

She shrugged and spread her hands, palms up.

"Religious zealot?"

She shook her head.

"Unusual family connections?"

"Damn it, Spenser, I don't know. If I knew, I'd tell you."

"Try picturing the circumstances when you got the impression he was unusual. Who said it? Where were you?"

She laughed. "Spenser, I can't do it. I don't remember. You're like a hammer after a nail."

"Sorry, I tend to get caught up in my work."

"I guess you do. You're a very interesting man. One might misjudge you. One might even underrate you, and I think that might be a very bad error."

"Underrate? Me?"

"Well, here you are a big guy with sort of a classy broken nose and clever patter. It would be easy to assume you were getting by on that. That maybe you were a little cynical and a little shallow. I half figured you got me in here just to make a pass at me. But I just saw you at work, and I would not want to be somebody you were really after."

"Now you're making me feel funny," I said. "Because half the reason I invited you in here was to make a pass at you."

"Maybe," she said and smiled. "But first you would work."

"Okay," I said. "I worked. I am a sleuth, and being a sleuth I can add two and two, blue eyes. If you half expected me to make a pass and you came anyway, then you must have half wanted me to do so . . . sweetheart."

"My eyes are brown."

"I know, but I can't do Bogart saying 'brown eyes.' And don't change the subject."

She took the final sip from her brandy glass and put it on the coffee table. When she did she was close to my face. "See?" she said looking at me steadily. "See how brown they are?"

"Black, I'd say. Closer to black."

I put my hands on either side of her face and kissed her on the mouth. She kissed me back. It was a long kiss, and when it ended I still held her face in my hands.

"Maybe you're right," she said. "Maybe they are more black than brown. Perhaps if you were to sit on the couch you might be able to see better."

I moved over. "Yes," I said, "this confirms my suspicion. Your eyes are black rather than brown."

She leaned forward and kissed me. I put my arms around her. She turned across my lap so I was holding her in my arms and put her arms around my neck. The kiss lasted longer than the first one and had some body English on it. I ran my hand under her sweater up along the depression of her spine, feeling the smooth muscles that ran parallel. We were lying now on the couch, and her mouth was open. I slid my hand back down along her spine and under the waistband of her pants. She groaned and arched her body against me, turning slightly as I moved my hand along the waistband toward the front zipper. I reached it and fumbled at it. Old surgeon's hands. She pulled back from the kiss, reached down, and took my hand away. I let her. We were gasping.

"No, Spenser," she managed. "Not the first time. Not in your apartment."

I didn't say anything. I couldn't think of anything to say, and I was concentrating on breathing.

"I know it's silly. But I can't get rid of upbringing; I can't get rid of momma saying that only dirty girls did it on the first date. I come from a different time."

"I know," I said. "I come from the same time." My voice was very hoarse. I cleared my throat. We continued to lie on the couch, my arm around her.

"There will be other times. Perhaps you'd like to try my cooking. In my house. I'm not cold, Spenser, and I would have been hurt if you hadn't tried, but not the first time. I just wouldn't like myself. Next time . . ."

"Yeah," I said. Clearing my throat hadn't helped, but I was getting my breathing under control. "I know. I'd love to try your cooking. What say we hop in the car and drive right out to your place now for a snack?"

She laughed. "You're not a quitter, are you."

"It's just that I may be suffering from terminal tumescence," I said.

She laughed again and sat up.

I said, "How about dinner together next week? That way you won't feel quite so hustled, maybe?"

She sat and looked down at me for some time. Her black hair falling forward around her face. Her lipstick smeared around her mouth. "You're quite nice, Spenser." She put her hand against my cheek for a moment. "Will you come and have dinner with me at my home next Tuesday evening at eight?"

"I will be very pleased to," I said.

We stood up. She put her hand out. I shook it. I walked to the door with her. She said, "Good night, Spenser."

I said, "Good night, Susan."

I opened the door for her, and she went out. I closed it. I breathed as much air as I could get into my lungs and let it out very slowly. Next time, I thought. Tuesday night. Dinner at her house. Hot dog.

10

Susan Silverman called me at my office at nine thirty the next morning.

"I've found out about that commune," she said.

"Tell me," I said.

"It's an old house in the woods back from Lowell Street near the Smithfield-Reading line."

"Can you tell me how to get there?"

"I'll take you."

"I was hoping you would. I'll be out in an hour."

"Come to my office," she said.

"At the school?" I said.

"Yes, what's wrong?"

"Mr. Moriarty might assault me with a ruler. I don't want to start up with no assistant principal."

"He probably won't recognize you without your white raincoat," she said. "The sun's out."

"Okay," I said, "I'll run the risk."

It was sunny, and the first hint of a New England fall murmured behind the sunshine. Warm enough for the top down on my convertible. Cold enough for a pale denim jacket. I drank a large paper cup of black coffee on the way and finished it just before I got to the Smithfield cutoff.

I found a space in the high school parking lot and went in.

The receptionist in the guidance office was in brown knit today and displaying a lot of cleavage. I admired it. She wasn't Susan Silverman, but she wasn't Lassie either, and there was little to be gained in elitist thinking.

Susan Silverman came out of her office with a red, blue, and green striped blazer on.

"I'll be back in about half an hour, Carla," she said to the redhead and to me. "Why don't we take my car? It'll be easier than giving you directions."

I said, "Okay," and we went out of the office and down a school corridor I hadn't walked before. But it was a school corridor. The smell of it and the long rows of lockers and the tone of repressed energy were like they always were. The guidance setup was different, though. Guidance counseling in my school meant the football coach banged your head against a locker and told you to shape up.

Susan Silverman said, "Were you looking down the front of my secretary's dress when I came out?"

"I was looking for clues," I said. "I'm a professional investigator."

She said, "Mmmm."

We went out a side door to the parking lot. Behind it the lawn stretched green to a football field ringed with new-looking bleachers and past that a line of trees. There was a group of girls in blue gym shorts and gold T-shirts playing field hockey under the eye of a lean tan woman in blue warm-up pants and a white polo shirt with a whistle in her mouth.

"Gym class?" I asked.

"Yes."

Susan's car was a two-year-old Nova. I opened the door for her, and she slipped into the seat, tucking her blue skirt under her.

We drove out of the parking lot, turned left toward the

center of town, and then right on Main Street and headed north.

"How'd you locate this place so quickly?"

"I collected a favor," she said, "from a girl in school."

We turned left off Main Street and headed east. The road was narrow, and the houses became sparser. Most of the road was through woods, and it seemed incredible that we were but fifteen miles from Boston and in the northern reaches of a megalopolis that stretched south through Richmond, Virginia. On my right was a pasture with black and white Ayrshire cows grazing behind a stone wall piled without benefit of mortar. Then more woods, mostly elm trees with birch trees gleaming through occasionally and a smattering of white pine.

"It's along here somewhere," she said.

"What are we looking for?"

"A dirt road on the left about a half mile past the cow pasture."

"There," I said, "just before the red maple."

She nodded and turned in. It was a narrow road, rocky and humpbacked beneath the wheel ruts. Tree branches scraped the sides and roof of the car as we drove. Dogberry bushes clustered along the edge of the path. A lot of rust-colored rock outcroppings showed among the greenery, and waxy-looking green vines grew among them in the shade, putting forth tiny blue flowers. All that waxy green effort for that reticent little flower.

We pulled around a bend about two hundred yards in and stopped. The land before us was cleared and might once have been a lawn. Now it was an expanse of gravel spattered with an occasional clump of weeds, some of which, coarse and sparse-leafed, looked waist-high. Behind one clump was a discarded bicycle on its back, its wheelless forks pointing up. The scavenged shell of a 1937 Hudson

Terraplane rusted quietly at the far edge of the clearing. The remnants of a sidewalk, big squares of cracked cement, heaved and buckled by frost, led up to a one-story house. Once, when it was newly built, an enthusiastic real estate broker might have listed it as a contemporary bungalow. It was a low ranch built on a slab. The siding was asphalt shingle faded now to a pale green. A peak over the front door had been vertically paneled with natural planks, and a scalloped molding, showing traces of pink paint, ran across the front. Attached to the house was a disproportionate cinder block carport, partly enclosed, as if the owner had given up and moved out in mid-mortar. From the carport came the steady whine of a gasoline engine. Not a car, maybe a generator. I saw no utility wires running in from the road.

A narrow mongrel bitch, about knee-high, with pendulous dugs, burrowed in an overturned trash barrel near the front door. A plump brown-haired girl of maybe fourteen sat on the front steps. She had big dark eyes that looked even bigger and darker in contrast with her white, doughy face. She had on a white T-shirt, blue dungarees with a huge flare at the bottom, and no shoes. She was eating a Twinkie and in her right hand held an open can of Coke and a burning filter tip cigarette. She looked at us without expression as we got out of the car and started up the walk.

"I don't like it here," Susan Silverman said.

"That's the trouble with you urban intellectuals," I said. "You have no sense of nature's subtle rhythms."

The girl finished her Twinkie as we reached her and washed it down with the rest of the Coke.

"Good morning," I said.

She looked at me without expression, inhaled most of her filter tip cigarette, and without taking it from her mouth, let the smoke out through her nose. Then she yelled, "Vic."

The screen door behind her scraped open—one hinge was loose—and out he came. Susan Silverman put her hand on my arm.

"You were right," I said. "He is unusual, isn't he?"

Vic Harroway was perhaps five ten, three inches shorter than I, and twenty pounds heavier. Say, 215. He was a body builder, but a body builder gone mad. He embodied every excess of body building that an adolescent fantasy could concoct. His hair was a bright cheap blond, cut straight across the forehead in a Julius Caesar shag. The muscles in his neck and chest were so swollen his skin looked as if it would burst over them. There were stretch marks pale against his dark tan where the deltoid muscles drape over the shoulder and stretch marks over his biceps and in the rigid valley between his pectoral muscles. His abdominal muscles looked like cobblestones. The white shorts were slit up the side to accommodate his thigh muscles. They too showed stretch marks. My stomach contracted at the amount of effort he'd expended, the number of weights he'd lifted to get himself in this state.

He said, "What do you turds want?" Down home hospitality.

I said, "We're looking for Walden Pond, you glib devil you."

"Well there ain't no Walden Pond around here, so screw."

"I just love the way your eyes snap when you're angry," I said.

"If you came out here looking for trouble, you're gonna find it, Jack. Take your slut and get your ass out of here, or I'll bend you into an earring."

I looked at Susan Silverman. "Slut?" I said.

Harroway said, "That's right. You don't like it? You want to make something out of it?" He jumped lightly off the steps and landed in front of me, maybe four feet away, slightly crouched. I could feel Susan Silverman lean back, but she didn't step back. A point for her. A point for me too, because as Harroway landed I brought my gun out, and as he went into his crouch he found himself staring into its barrel. I held it straight out in front of me, level with his face.

"Let's not be angry with each other, Vic. Let us reason together," I said.

"What the hell is this? What do you want?"

"I am looking for a boy named Kevin Bartlett. I came out here to ask if you'd seen him."

"I don't know anybody named Kevin Bartlett."

"How about the young lady," I asked, still looking at Harroway. "Do you know Kevin Bartlett?"

"No." I heard a match strike and smelled the cigarette smoke as she lit up. Imperturbable.

The generator in the garage whined on. The dog found a bone and was crunching on it vigorously. There was color on Harroway's cheekbones; he looked as if he had a fever. I was stymied. I wanted to search the place, but I didn't want to turn my back on Harroway. I didn't want to have to herd him and the girl around with me. I didn't want Susan out of my sight. I was trespassing, which bothered me a bit. And I had no reason not to believe them. I didn't know who might be in the house or behind it or in the garage.

"If at first you don't succeed," I said to Susan Silverman, "the hell with it. Come on."

We backed down the sidewalk to her car and got in. Harroway never took his eyes off me as we went. Susan U-turned on the lawn, and we drove away. Another point for Susan. She didn't spin gravel getting out of there.

She didn't say anything, but I noticed her knuckles were

white on the steering wheel. When we got back to Main Street, she pulled over to the side of the road and stopped.

"I feel sick," she said. She kept her hands on the wheel and stared straight ahead. She was shivering as if it were cold. "My God, what a revolting creature he was. My God! Like a . . . like a rhinoceros or something. A kind of impenetrable brutality."

I put a hand on her shoulder and didn't say anything.

We sat maybe two minutes that way. Then she put the car in gear again. "I'm okay," she said.

"I'll say."

"What do you think?" she said. "Did you learn anything?"

I shrugged. "I learned where that place is and what Vic Harroway is like. I don't know if Kevin is there or not."

"It seemed like an unpleasant experience for nothing," she said.

"Well, that's my line of work. I go look at things and see what happens. If they were lying, maybe they will do some things because I went there today. Maybe they will make a mistake. The worst thing in any case is when nothing is happening. It's like playing tennis: you just keep returning the ball until somebody makes a mistake. Then you see."

She shook her head. "What if you hadn't had a gun?"

"I usually have a gun."

"But, my God, if you hadn't, or you hadn't reached it in time?"

"I don't know," I said. "It depends on how good Harroway really is. He looks good. But guys that look like that often don't have to fight. Who's going to start up with them? There's a lot to being strong, but there's a lot to knowing how. Maybe someday we'll find out if Harroway knows how."

She looked at me and frowned. "You want to, don't you?

You want to fight him. You want to see if you can beat him."

"I didn't like that 'slut' remark."

"Jesus Christ," she said. "You adolescent, you. Do you think it matters to me if someone like Vic Harroway calls me a slut? Next thing you'll challenge him to a duel." She wheeled the car into the high school parking lot and braked sharply.

I grinned at her boyishly, or maybe adolescently.

She put her hand on my forearm. "Don't mess with him, Spenser," she said. "You looked . . ." she searched for a word, "frail beside him."

"Well, anyway," I said, "I'm sorry you had to go. If I'd known, I'd have left you home."

She smiled at me, her even white teeth bright in her tan face. "Spenser," she said, "you are a goddamned fool."

"You think so too, huh?" I said and got out.

11

That afternoon I was in the ID section of the Boston Police Department trying to find out if Vic Harroway had a record. If he did, the Boston cops didn't know about it. Neither did I.

It was almost five o'clock when I left police headquarters on Berkeley Street and drove to my office. The commuters were out, and the traffic was heavy. It took me fifteen minutes, and my office wasn't worth it. It was stale and hot when I unlocked the door. The mail had accumulated in a pile under the mail slot in the door. I stepped over it and went across the room to open the window. A spider had spun a symmetrical web across one corner of the window recess. I was careful not to disturb it. Every man needs a pet. I picked up the mail and sat at my desk to read it. Mostly bills and junk mail. No letter announcing my election to the Hawkshaw Hall of Fame. No invitation to play tennis with Bobby Riggs in the Astrodome. There was a note on pale violet stationery from a girl named Brenda Loring suggesting a weekend in Provincetown in the late fall when the tourists had gone home. I put that aside to answer later.

I called my answering service. They reported five calls

from Margery Bartlett during the afternoon. I said thank you, hung up, and dialed the Bartlett number.

"Where on earth have you been?" Margery Bartlett said when I told her who I was. "I've been trying to get you all afternoon."

"I was up to the Boston Athenaeum browsing through the collected works of Faith Baldwin," I said.

"Well, we need you out here, right away. My life has been threatened."

"Cops there?"

"Yes, there's a patrolman here now. But we want you here right away. Someone has threatened my life. Threatened to kill me. You get right out here, Spenser, right away."

"Yes, ma'am," I said, "right away."

I hung up, looked at my watch—five twenty—got up, closed the window, and headed for Smithfield. It was six fifteen when I got there. A Smithfield police cruiser was parked facing the street in the driveway. Paul Marsh, the patrolman I'd met before, was sitting in it, his head tipped back against the headrest, his cap tilted forward. The barrel end of a pump-action shotgun showed through the windshield held upright by a clip lock on the dashboard. I could hear the soft rush of open air on the police radio in the car as I stopped at the open side window near the driver.

"What's happening?" I asked.

He shook his head. "Phone call. Mrs. Bartlett answered and was threatened. Something about evening the score. I didn't talk to her. Trask did. He knows the details. I don't. This was my day off."

"You eaten?"

"No, but one of the guys'll bring me down something in a while."

"I'll be here if you want to shoot out and get something."

Marsh shook his head again. "Naw, Trask would have my ass. I think he's hot for Mrs. Bartlett."

"Okay," I said. "I'll go in and see what she can tell me. Her husband home?"

"Nope. He's still working. I guess. Just her and her daugther and the lawyer, Maguire."

They were in the kitchen. Maguire, small, neat, and worried, let me in. Marge Bartlett in a green crepe pants suit and white shirt with ruffled cuffs was standing against the kitchen counter turning a highball glass in her hands. She was very carefully made-up. At the kitchen table was the same young girl I'd seen going for a swim on my first visit. The Bartletts' daughter, I assumed. She was eating a macaroni and cheese TV dinner and drinking a can of Tab. Her bones were small, her face was delicate and impassive. Her black hair was long and straight. She was wearing a faded yellow sweat shirt that said Make Love Not War in black letters across the front. The Lab sat on the floor by her chair and watched every mouthful as it moved from the foil container to her mouth.

Marge Bartlett said, "Spenser, where the hell were you?"

"You already asked me that," I said.

Maguire said, "Glad you got here, Spenser."

Marge Bartlett said, "They threatened me. They said they'd ..." She glanced at her daughter. "Dolly, why don't you finish your supper and go watch TV in the den?"

"Oh, Ma ... I know what they said. I heard you talking about it with Mr. Trask this afternoon." She drank some Tab.

"Well you shouldn't have. You shouldn't be hearing that sort of thing."

"Oh, Ma."

"What exactly happened, Mrs. Bartlett?" I asked.

"They called about noon," she said.

"Did you record it?"

Maguire said, "No. They took the recorder off this morning about three hours before the call."

"Okay," I said, "what did they say? Be careful and get it as exact as possible."

Dolly said, "Ma, is there any dessert?"

"I don't know. Look in the cupboard and don't interrupt." She turned toward me. "The call came about noon. I was in the study running over my lines. I'm playing Desdemona in a production of *Othello* we're putting on in town. And the phone rang and I answered it. Hoping it might be about Kevin, and a girl's voice said, 'We got Kevin, now we're going to even it up with you. We're going to shoot you in the . . .' and she used a dirty word. It refers to the female sex area. Do you know which one I mean? It starts with *c*." She glanced at her daughter.

"Yeah, I know the word. Anything else?"

"No. She just said that and hung up. Why would she say that?"

I shrugged. Dolly Bartlett got a package of Nutter Butter cookies from the cabinet and another Tab from the refrigerator and sat back down at the table.

"And you didn't recognize the voice?"

"No."

Maguire poured a stiff shot into the glass, added ice and soda, and gave it to Marge Bartlett.

"When you say girl's voice, how old a girl?"

"Oh, a girl. You know, not a woman, a teenager."

Dolly Bartlett said, "Ma, why don't you ever get Coke. I hate Tab."

"Dolly, damn it, will you not interrupt me? Don't you realize that I'm under great stress? You might have a little consideration. The Tab has almost no calories. Don't you care that I'm in danger? Great danger?" Tears began to form, and her lower lip began to quiver. "Oh, goddamn you," she said and hustled out of the room without spilling her drink.

Maguire said, "Aw, Marge, c'mon," rolled his eyeballs at me, and hustled out after her. Dolly Bartlett continued to eat her Nutter Butter cookies.

"My name is Spenser," I said. "I gather you're Dolly."

"Yes," she said. "My name is really Delilah. Isn't that a dumb name?"

"Yeah," I said, "Delilah is kind of dumb."

"Want a cookie?"

I took one. "Thank you."

"You're welcome. Want any Tab?"

"No, thank you." The cookie tasted like a peanut-flavored matchbook.

"She lied to you, you know," Dolly said.

"Your mother?"

"Yes."

"How do you know?"

"I listened upstairs on the other phone. I do it all the time. If you pick it up before she does, she never notices. She's really dumb."

"What did the girl really say when she called?"

"She said they were going to punish my mother for screwing her ass off all over town," Dolly said. She offered Punkin a Nutter Butter cookie. He sniffed it and refused. My respect for him increased. "Then the girl said that about shooting her down there. Isn't that gross?"

"Gross," I said.

"Don't tell my mother I told you."

"I won't. Did the girl say anything else?"

"No."

"Do you think what she said about your mother was

true?" That was a nice touch; grill the kid about her mother's sex habits. Nice line of work you're in, Spenser.

"Oh sure. Everybody knows about my mother except maybe Daddy. She screws with everybody. She screws with Mr. Trask, I know."

I wanted to know who else but couldn't bring myself to ask. Instead I said, "Does it bother you?"

"Yeah, of course, but," she shrugged, "you get used to it, you know?"

"I guess you would, wouldn't you."

"Used to drive Kevin crazy, though. I don't know if he ever got used to it like I did."

"It's harder for boys to get used to, maybe," I said. It wasn't too easy for me to get used to. Maybe I should become a florist.

She shrugged again.

Her mother came back into the kitchen, her eyes puffy, with fresh makeup around them. Earl Maguire came with her. Was she screwing with him? Screwing with Mr. Trask? Christ.

Marge Bartlett said, "Dolly, go in the den and watch TV, please, darling. Mommy is upset. It will be better for you to go in there now." She kissed her daughter on top of her head. Dolly picked up the package of cookies. "Come on, Punkin," she said, and the dog followed her out of the kitchen.

"Well, Mr. Spenser, I see you've met my Dolly. Did you and she have a nice talk?"

"Yep."

"Good. Chief Trask has left a patrolman here to guard the house. But I'd feel much safer if you'd stay too."

Earl Maguire said, "We'd expect to pay you extra, of course. Mrs. Bartlett has already talked to her husband, and Rog has authorized payment to you."

"What can I do the cops can't?"

"You can stay close to me," Mrs. Bartlett said. "You can go with me when I shop and go to parties and play rehearsal and things. You can be right here in the house."

"We'd be employing you as a bodyguard," Maguire said.

"While I'm guarding your body, I can't be looking for your kid," I said.

"Just for a little while," she said. "Please? For me?"

"Okay. I'll have to go home and pack a suitcase. You'll be all right with Marsh here. Just stay close till I come back. This may just be a crank call, you know. Kidnappings and disappearances bring out a lot of crank calls."

12

One of the good parts of living alone is when you move out no one minds. It's also one of the bad parts. I went home, packed, and was back at the Bartletts' in an hour and a half.

Roger Bartlett was home from work, and he installed me in a bedroom on the second floor. It was a big pleasant room, paneled in pine planking stained an ice-blue. The ceiling was beamed in a crisscross pattern; there was a wide-board floor and a big closet with folding louvered doors and a bureau built in behind them. There was a double bed with a Hitchcock headboard and a patchwork quilt, a pine Governor Winthrop desk, and a wooden rocker with arms and a rush seat that had been done in an antique-blue and stenciled in gold. There was a blue and red braided rug on the floor, and the drapes on the windows were a red and blue print featuring Revolutionary War scenes. Very nice.

"You eat supper yet?" Roger Bartlett asked.

"No."

"Me either. Come on down and we'll rustle up a litle grub. Gotta eat to live, right?" I nodded.

"Gotta eat to live," he repeated and headed downstairs.

A portable TV on the kitchen counter was showing a ball game. The Sox were playing the Angels, and neither was a contender. It was nearly the end of the season, and the announcers and the crowd noise reflected that fact. There is nothing quite like the sound of a pointless ball game late in the season. It is a very nostalgic sound. Sunday afternoon, early fall, car radio, beach traffic.

Bartlett handed me a can of beer, and I sipped it looking at the ball game. Order and pattern, discernible goals strenuously sought within rigidly defined rules. A lot of pressure and a lot of grace, but no tragedy. The Summer Game.

"What do you think about this stuff, Spenser? What's going on?" Bartlett was cutting slices of breast meat from a roast turkey. "I mean, where's my kid? Why does someone want to kill my wife? What the hell have I ever done to anybody?"

"I was going to ask you," I said.

"What do you mean?"

"I mean this whole thing smells of revenge. It smells of harassment. It just doesn't feel right as a kidnapping. The time between the disappearance and the ransom demand. The peculiar note. The peculiar phone call. The trick with the coffin—someone put a lotta work into that. Now the threatening phone call—if it's not just a crank. Someone doesn't like you or your wife or both."

"But who the hell . . ." Marge Bartlett came in carrying the highball glass. Her lipstick was fresh and her hair was combed and her eye shadow looked newly applied. She poked the glass at her husband. "Fill 'er up," she said and giggled. "Fill 'er up. Or is there a fuel shortage?"

"Why don't you slow down, Marge?" Bartlett said. He took the glass.

"Slow down. Slow down. That's all you can say. Slow down. Well I'm not going to slow down. Live fast, die young, and have a good-looking corpse. That's my motto." She did a pirouette and bumped against the counter.

"Everything is slow down with you, Roger. Old slow-down-Roger, that's you."

Bartlett gave her a new drink.

"You want mayonnaise?" He asked me.

"Please," I said. He put a plate of sliced turkey, a jar of mayonnaise, some bread-and-butter pickles, and a loaf of oatmeal bread on the table. "Help yourself," he said.

"My God, Roger," Marge Bartlett said. "Is that how you're going to feed him? No plate? No napkins? Can't you even make a salad? We have those nice mugs for beer that Dolly and I bought you."

"It's a lot better than the way you're feeding him," Bartlett answered. "Or me."

"Oh, certainly. I should be cooking a big meal when my very life has been threatened. I should be keeping your supper warm in the oven when you won't even come home from work to protect me."

"Christ! Trask was here and Paul Marsh and Earl. I was way the hell and gone out past Worcester on a job."

"Well, why don't you work closer to home, anyway? You're never around when I need you."

"I can't find enough work close to home to pay for all the goddamned scotch you drink."

"You bastard," she said and threw her drink at him. A little scotch spattered on my turkey sandwich. Not a bad combination.

"Oh, stop showing off for Spenser," Bartlett said. He got a paper towel and wiped up the moisture on the table. She made a new drink.

"I'm sorry, Mr. Spenser. It's just that I'm under great strain, as you might imagine. I'm an artist. I'm volatile; I'm quick to anger."

"Yeah," I said, "both those things. You got a lousy arm, though. You got scotch on my sandwich."

She drank half her drink. Not only her face but her whole body seemed to get progressively slacker as she drank. Her voice got harsher, while her language got more affected. I wondered if the progress continued until she sank to the floor screaming nonsense. I didn't think I'd find out. I was pretty sure I'd crack first.

"Can you think of any connection between this death threat and Kevin's disappearance?" Slick how smoothly I changed the subject.

"I think someone is out to get us," she said. Oddly, I agreed with her. It made me nervous.

"Who the hell would be out to get us?" Bartlett said. "We haven't got any enemies."

"How about in business? Got anyone mad at you there? Fire anyone? Out-shrewd someone?"

He shook his head. His wife said, "Not good old Rog. Everybody likes good old Rog. Everyone thinks he's so terrific. Everyone feels sorry for him married to a bitch. But I know him. The bastard."

"How about you?" I said to her. "Anyone you can think of that has reason to hate you? Or hates you without reason?" She looked at me blankly. The booze was weaving its magic spell. "Any old boyfriends, disappointed lovers?"

"No"—she shook her head angrily—"of course not."

"Can either of you think of anyone at all who hates you enough to give you this kind of trouble?" Blank stares. "There must be someone. Maybe hate is too strong a word. Who dislikes you the most of anyone you know?"

In a voice thick and furry with booze she said, "Kevin."

Bartlett said, "Marge, for God's sake."

"It's true," she said. "The little sonova bitch hates us."

"Marge, goddamn you. You leave my kid alone. He didn't kidnap himself."

"The little sonova bitch." She was mumbling now.

"She's drunk as a goddamned skunk, Spenser. I'm putting her to bed. Drunk as a skunk." He took her arm, and she sagged protestingly away from him. "Sonova bitch." She began to giggle. "He's the little sonova bitch, and you're the big sonova bitch." She sat down on the floor still giggling. I got up.

"You need any help?" I said.

He shook his head. "I've done this before."

"Okay, then I'll go to bed. Thanks for supper." As I went out of the kitchen I saw Dolly Bartlett scuttle up the stairs ahead of me and into her room. Pleasant dreams, kid.

13

The next morning, Saturday, Kevin's guinea pig turned up. I was sitting at the kitchen table reading the *Globe* when I heard Marge Bartlett scream in the front hall. A short startled scream and then a long steady one. When I got there the front door was ajar, and she was holding an open package about the size of a shoe box. I took it from her. Inside was a dead guinea pig on its back, its short legs sticking stiffly up. I looked out the door. A young Smithfield cop I didn't know came busting around the corner of the house with a shotgun at high port.

"It's okay," I said. Marge Bartlett continued to scream steadily. Now that I was holding the package her hands were free, and she put both of them over her face. The cop came in holding the shotgun down along the side of his leg, the muzzle pointing at the floor. He looked in the box and made a face. "Jesus Christ," he said.

"It came in the mail," I said. "I suppose it's the same one the kid took with him when he disappeared."

Marge Bartlett stopped screaming. She nodded without taking her hands from her face. The cop said, "I'll call Trask," and headed back for the cruiser in the driveway. I took the box and wrapping paper and dead guinea pig into the kitchen and sat down at the table and looked at them.

There was nothing to suggest what killed the guinea pig. The box said Thom McAn on the cover, and the brown paper in which it had been wrapped looked like all the other brown paper wrapping in the world. The box had been mailed in Boston, addressed to Mrs. Margery Bartlett. There was no return address. They're too smart for me, I thought.

"What does it mean, Spenser?" Marge Bartlett asked.

"I don't know. Just more of the same. I'd guess the guinea pig died, and someone thought it would be a good idea to send it to you. It doesn't look as if it's been killed. That might suggest that Kevin is well."

"Why?"

"Well, a kidnapper or a murderer is not likely to bother keeping a guinea pig, right?"

She nodded. I heard a car spin gravel into the driveway and slam to a stop. I bet myself it was Trask. I won. He came in without knocking.

"Oh, George," Marge Bartlett said, "I can't stand much more."

He crossed to where she was standing and put an arm around her shoulder. "Marge, we're doing what we can. We're working on it around the clock." He looked at me. "Where's the evidence?"

I nodded at the box on the table.

"You been messing with it?" Trask said. Tough as nails.

"Not me, Chief. I've been keeping it under close surveillance. I think the guinea pig is faking."

"Move aside," he said and picked up the box. He looked at the guinea pig and shook his head. "Sick," he said. "Sickest goddamned thing I ever been involved in. Hey, Silveria." The young cop appeared at the back door. He had a round moon face and bushy black hair. His uniform cap seemed too small for his head.

"Take this stuff down to the station and hold it for me. I'll be down in a while to examine it. Send Marsh back here to relieve you."

Silveria departed. Trask took a ball-point pen and a notebook out of his shirt pocket. "Okay, Marge," he said, "let's have it all. When did the package arrive?" I didn't need to dance that circle with them. "Excuse me," I said and went out the back door. The day was new and sunny. All it needed to be September Morn was a nude bathing in the pool. I looked, just to be sure, but there wasn't any. A scarlet tanager flashed across the lawn from the crab apple tree to the barn and disappeared into an open loft where the fake post for a hay hoist that never existed jutted out over the door.

I walked over to the barn. Inside was a collection of power mowers, hedge trimmers, electric clippers, rollers, lawn sweepers, barrels, paint cans, posthole diggers, shovels, rakes, bicycle parts, several kegs of eight-penny nails, some folding lawn chairs, a hose, snow tires, and a beach umbrella. To the right a set of stairs ascended to the loft. On the first step Dolly Bartlett was sitting listening to a portable radio through an earplug. She was eating Fritos from a plastic bag. The dog sat on the floor beside her with his mouth open and his tongue hanging out, panting.

"Good morning," I said.

"Hi." She offered the bag of Fritos to me. I took one and ate it. It wasn't as bad as some things I'd eaten. The Nutter Butter cookies, for instance.

"Had breakfast?" I really know how to talk to kids. After that I could ask her how she was doing in school, or maybe her age. Really get her on my side.

She shook her head and nodded at the Fritos.

"You'd be better off eating the bag," I said.

She giggled. "I bet I wouldn't," she said.

"Maybe not," I said. "Bags aren't nourishing anymore. Now when I was a boy . . ."

She made a face and stuck out her tongue. "Oh," I said, "you heard that line before?"

She nodded. I was competing with the top forty sounds in Boston playing loud in her earphone, and she was only half-listening to me. That was okay because I was only half-saying anything.

"You want to see Kevin's hideout?" she said, one ear still fastened to the radio.

"Yes," I said.

"Come on." She got up carrying the radio and headed up the stairs. Punkin and I scrambled for second position. I won. Still got the old reflexes.

The second floor of the barn was unfinished. Exposed beams, subflooring. At one end a small room had been studded off and Sheetrock nailed up. Some carpenter tools lay on the floor near it, and a box of blue lathing nails had spilled on the floor. It looked like a project Roger Bartlett was going to do in his spare time, and he didn't have any spare time. There was scrap lumber and Sheetrock trimmings in a pile as if someone had swept them up and gone for a trash barrel and been waylaid. A number of four-by-eight plywood panels in a simulated wood-plank texture were leaning against a wall.

"In here," Dolly said. And disappeared into the studded-off room. I followed. It was probably going to be a bathroom from the size and the rough openings that looked to be for plumbing. A makeshift partition had been constructed out of some paneling and two sawhorses. Behind it was a steamer trunk and a low canvas lawn chair. The steamer trunk was locked with a padlock. The floor was covered with a rug that appeared to be a remnant of wall-to-wall carpeting. The window looked out over the pool and the back of the house. The wiring was in, and a bare light bulb was screwed into a porcelain receptacle. A string hung from it.

"What's in the trunk?" I asked.

"I don't know. Kevin always kept it locked up. He never let me in here."

"Do your mother and father know about this place?"

"I doubt it. My father hasn't worked up here since last summer, and my mother's never been up here. She says it should be fixed up so she can have it for a studio. But she hasn't ever come up. Just me and Kevin, and Kevin always kicked me out when he came up here. He didn't want anyone to know about his place."

"How come you're telling me?"

She shrugged. "You're a detective."

I nodded. I was glad she said that because I was beginning to have my doubts.

"You get along with Kevin?" I asked.

"He's creepy," she said, "but he's okay sometimes." She shrugged again. "He's my brother. I've known him all my life."

"Okay, Dolly, here's what I'm going to do. I'm going to break into that trunk. Maybe it won't have anything that will help, but maybe it will, and the only way to know is to look. I know it's not mine, but maybe it will help us find Kevin, all right?"

"Kevin will be mad."

"I won't tell him about your being here."

"Okay."

I found a pinch bar among the tools on the floor and pried the hasp off the trunk. Inside the cover of the trunk an eight-by-ten glossy was attached with adhesive tape, a publicity still of Vic Harroway in a body-building pose. In the trunk itself was a collection of body-building magazines, a scrapbook, a pair of handsprings that you squeezed to build up your grip, and two thirty-pound dumbbells.

Dolly did an exaggerated shudder. "Gross," she said.

"What?" I said.

"The guy in the picture. Ugh!"

"Do you know him?" I asked.

"No."

I sat down in the lawn chair and picked up the first magazine in the pile. Dolly said, "Are you going to read that?"

I said, "I'm going to read them all."

"Sick," she said.

"They're clues. That's what I'm supposed to do—study clues and after studying enough of them I'm supposed to solve a mystery and . . ."

"Are you going to tell?" she said.

I knew what she meant. Kevin had hidden this stuff from his parents, for whatever reason.

"No," I said. "Are you?"

"No."

I opened a copy of *Strength and Health*. On the inside cover and spilling over onto page 1, there was an ad for high-protein health food and pictures of hugely muscled people who apparently ate it. There were badly laid-out ads for strength-training booklets, weight-lifting equipment, and choker bathing suits; and pictures of weight lifters and Mr. America contestants. On page 39 was a sepia-tone picture of Vic Harroway. He had on a white bikini and was posed on a beach in front of a low shelf of rock that kicked spray up as the sea hit it. His right arm was flexed to show the biceps. His left hand was clamped behind his neck, and he was flexed forward with his right knee bent and the toes of his left leg barely touching the ground. The sun glistened on his features, and his narrowed eyes were fixed on something high and distant and doubtless grand behind the camera. Beauty is its own excuse for being. The caption said, "Vic Harroway, Mr. Northeastern America, Combines Weight Lifting and Yoga." I read the story. It said the same thing in supermasculine prose that made me want to run out and uproot a tree.

While I read, Dolly Bartlett sat down against the wall with her knees drawn up to her chest and listened to her radio.

I went through all the strength magazines. They dated back five years, and each of them had a story on Vic Harroway. I learned how Vic trained down for "that polished look." I learned Vic's diet-supplement secrets for gaining "ten to fifteen pounds of solid muscles." I learned Vic's technique for developing "sinewy and shapely under-pinnings." I didn't learn much about Vic's theories on kidnapping and harassment or if he might know where Kevin Bartlett was.

I looked at the scrapbook. It was what I thought it would be. Clippings of Vic Harroway's triumphs in body-building contests. Ads announcing the opening of a new health spa where Vic Harroway would be the supervisor of physical conditioning. Fifteen-year-old newspaper clippings of Vic Harroway as a high school football hero in Everett. Snapshots of Vic and one of Vic and Kevin with Vic's arm around Kevin's shoulder. Harroway was smiling. Kevin looked very serious.

"Did Kevin lift weights?" I asked Dolly.

"No. I remember he wanted to buy a set once, but my mother wouldn't let him."

"Why not?"

"I don't know. She said it would make him big and beefy and stuff, you know?"

I nodded.

"They had a big fight about it."

I nodded again.

"Would it?"

"Would it what?"

"Would it make him big and beefy?"

"Not if he did it right," I said. I took the publicity shot of Harroway, put the magazines and the scrapbook back in the trunk, and closed it. Dolly and the dog and I went downstairs. The dog edged me out on the way down, and I was last. In the driveway Marge Bartlett was standing looking impatiently into the open barn. She had on a pale violet pants suit with huge cuffed bell-bottoms and blunt-nosed black shoes poking out underneath. A big burlap purse with a crocheted design hung from her shoulder. She wore white lipstick, and her nails were polished in a pale lavender.

"Come on, Dolly, time to go to Aunt Betty's. Hop in the car."

"Aw, Ma, I don't want to go over there again."

"Come on now, no arguing. Hop in the car. I've got a lot of shopping to do. The party is tonight, and I don't want you in the way. You know how nervous I get when I'm having a big party. And while I'm at the shopping center I don't want you here alone. It's too dangerous."

I went to my car and put the photo in the glove compartment.

"Well, lemme stay with Mr. Spenser."

Marge Bartlett shook her head firmly. "Not on your life. Mr. Spenser is my bodyguard, and he'll have to go with me to the shopping center." She clapped her hands once, sharply. "In the car."

Dolly climbed into the backseat of the red Mustang. Marge Bartlett got in behind the wheel, and I sat beside her.

The dog stood in front of the car with his ears back and stared at us.

"Can I bring Punkin?" Dolly asked.

"Absolutely not. I don't want him getting the car all muddy, and Aunt Betty can't stand dogs anyway."

"He's not muddy," Dolly said.

The cop in the Smithfield cruiser poked his head out the side window and said, "Where you going?"

"It's all right. Mr. Spenser is with me. We'll be gone most of the day, shopping."

"Whoopee," I said. "All day."

The cop nodded. "Okay, Mrs. Bartlett. I'm going to take off then. You let us know when you're back, and Chief'll send someone up."

He started the cruiser and headed down the drive. We followed. He turned left. We turned right.

14

The north shore shopping center was on high ground north off Route 128 in Peabody. Red brick, symmetrical evergreens, and parking for eight thousand cars. I discovered that Marge Bartlett was a member of the shopping center the way some people belong to a country club. Between ten fifteen and one twenty she charged $375 worth of clothes. I spent that time watching her, nodding approval when she asked my opinion, keeping a weather eye out for assailants, and trying not to look like a pervert as I stood around outside a series of ladies' dressing rooms. I was glad I hadn't worn my white raincoat. There were a lot of very well-shaped suburban ladies shopping in the same stores. Suburban ladies tended to wear their clothes quite snug, I noticed. I was alert for concealed weapons.

We got back to Smithfield at about a quarter of two. The house was still. Roger Bartlett worked Saturdays, and Dolly was going to spend the night with Aunt Betty. Punkin lay placidly in a hollow under some bushes to the right of the back door. Marge Bartlett held the door for me as I carried in the shopping bags. The dog came in behind us.

"Put them on the couch in the living room," she said. "I want to call the caterer."

There was a corpse in the living room. On the floor, face

down, with its head at a funny angle. I dropped the shopping bags and went back to the kitchen with my gun out.

Marge Bartlett was still on the phone with her back to me. No one was in sight. The back door was closed. The dog had settled under the kitchen table. I turned back to the living room and stood in the center, beside the corpse, and held my breath and listened. Except for Marge Bartlett talking with animation about a jellied salad, there was no sound.

I put the gun back in the hip holster and squatted down beside the corpse and looked at its face. It had been Earl Maguire. That's it for the law practice, Earl. I picked up one hand and bent the forefinger back and forth. He was cold and getting stiff. I put the hand down. All the college and all the law school and all the cramming for the bar, and someone snaps your neck for you when you're not much more than thirty. I looked around the room. A glass-topped rug was bunched toward Maguire's body. A fireplace poker lay maybe two feet beyond Maguire's outflung hand. An abstract oil painting was on the floor beneath a picture hook on the wall as if it had fallen.

I duck-walked over to the poker and looked at it without touching it. There was no sign of blood on it. I stood up and went to the front door. The lock button in the middle of the knob was in. The door was locked. I'd seen Marge Bartlett unlock the back door. I opened the front door. No sign of it being jimmied. There'd been no sign of jimmying on the back door. I'd have noticed when we came in. There weren't any other doors. I walked across the front hall to the dining room. It was undisturbed except that the door to the liquor cabinet was open. There was a lot of booze inside. It didn't look as if any was missing.

I heard Marge Bartlett hang up. I headed for the kitchen and cut her off before she got to the door.

"Stay here," I said.

"Why?"

"Earl Maguire is dead in your living room."

"My God, the party's in six hours."

"Inconsiderate bastard, wasn't he," I said.

She opened her mouth and then put both hands over it and pressed and didn't say anything. "Sit there," I said and steered her to a kitchen chair. She kept her hands over her mouth and watched me minutely while I called the cops. When she heard me say Maguire's neck was broken, she made a muffled squeak.

Five minutes later Trask arrived with a bald, fat old geezer who carried a black bag like the ones doctors used to carry when they made house calls. He eased himself down on his knees beside the body and looked at it. He was too fat to squat.

"When'd he die, Doc?" Trask had a notebook out and held a yellow Bic Banana pen poised over it to record the answer.

The doctor was strained for breath, kneeling down like that; it didn't help his temperament. "Before we got here," he said.

Trask got a little redder. "I know that, goddamn it. What I want to know is how long before we got here?"

"How the hell do I know, George? I don't even know what killed him, yet. His neck looks broken." The doctor picked up Maguire's head and turned it back and forth. A dark bruise ran along his cheek from the earlobe to the corner of his mouth. "Yep, neck's broken."

"What time you find him, Spenser?" Trask decided to question me. It wasn't going well with the doctor.

"Quarter of two."

"Exactly?"

"Approximately."

"Well, goddamn it, can't you be more exact? You're supposed to be some kind of hot stuff. I want to know the exact time of the discovery of the deceased. It could be vital."

"Only in the movies, Trask."

Trask looked past me and said, "Hello, Lieutenant." I turned and it was Healy. He had on the same straw hat with the big headband that I'd seen him in before. His jacket was gray tweed with a muted red line forming squares in it. Gray slacks, white shirt with a button-down collar, and a narrow black knit tie. Tan suede desert boots. He had his hands in his hip pockets, and his face was without expression as he looked down at the body.

"Worse and worse," he said.

Trask said, "This is Doc Woodson, Lieutenant. He was just saying that Maguire died of a broken neck."

"No, I didn't, George. I said his neck was broken. I didn't say it killed him."

"Well, it didn't help him none. That's for damned certain," Trask said.

Healy said, "When can you give me a report on him, Doctor Woodson?"

"We'll take him down Union Hospital now, and I can have something for you by, say, suppertime." He looked at me. "Gimme a hand up, young fella; you look strong enough." I helped him up. The effort left him red-faced, and there was sweat on his forehead. "Don't get the exercise I should," he said.

"Who found the body?" Healy asked.

Trask said, "Spenser," and jerked his head in my direction. I got the feeling he wished I were the body.

"Okay, tell me about it." Healy squatted down on his

heels beside the corpse and looked at it while I told him.

"Doors locked when you got here?"

"Yep, both of them. Mrs. Bartlett opened the back door with a key, and the front door was locked. I checked it."

"Let's check again," Healy said. We walked to the front door. Healy opened it, went outside, shut it behind him, and tried the knob. Locked. I opened it for him from the inside. We went to the back door. Healy did the same thing. Same result. I let him in. We walked around looking at the windows. Most of them were closed and locked. Those that weren't locked were screened. There was no sign they'd been tampered with. The screens were aluminum, part of screen and storm combinations.

"Someone could have gone out, reached back in, released the catches, and lowered the screen," I said, "to make it look like it was inside business."

Healy nodded absently. "Yeah," he said, "but why would someone do that?"

"Misdirect the cops," I said.

"Maybe," Healy said.

" 'Course with Chief Trask on the track," I said, "you probably don't need too much misdirection."

Healy separated a peppermint Life Saver from the roll and popped it into his mouth. He didn't offer me one. "Well, he's just a hick cop. Not a high-powered fast gun in from the city. Couldn't even solve a simple missing person squeal." He sucked on the Life Saver. "You find the kid yet?"

"Nope."

Healy said, "Oh."

We went back to the living room. The photographs had been taken. The measurements made. The corpse was wrapped in a blanket and lying on a stretcher. Trask looked at Healy. Healy nodded and Trask said, "Okay, let's get him out of here."

Two Smithfield cops picked up the stretcher and went out the front door.

"Union Hospital," Trask yelled after them. "And tell 'em it's for Doc Woodson when you get there."

"Anything missing, Trask?" Healy asked.

"Mrs. Bartlett says no. She don't see anything gone. Liquor cabinet was open but nothing missing."

Marge Bartlett was sitting with her knees pressed together on the couch. The lines around her mouth seemed to have deepened. She needed to freshen her makeup.

"What was he doing here, Mrs. Bartlett?" Healy said.

"Who?"

"Maguire. What was Maguire doing in your house while you were away?"

"Oh, Earl has his own key. He's an old and dear friend. He often lets himself in. We're having a party tonight, and he said he'd come out early and help me set up the bar and things because Roger wouldn't be able to get home till after supper. Almost time for . . . My God"—she looked at her watch—"it's after four. My company is coming in three and a half hours. I've got to get ready. Spenser, you're going to have to help me."

I nodded. Healy said, "Do you have any idea, Mrs. Bartlett, who might have done this?"

"To Earl? I don't know. He was a lawyer; perhaps he made enemies." She shrugged. "I don't know. Lieutenant, I simply must get ready. I'm having sixty-five people here tonight. And I'm already very late." She was on her feet moving toward the hall as she spoke.

Healy looked at her with a puzzled expression. "It's grief, Lieutenant," I said. "She's hiding her grief and carrying on."

Healy snorted. Trask said, "Well, she is. She's being damned brave."

"Brave," Healy said.

"I'll question her later on," Trask said, "when she's gotten herself together more. Ya know."

"Yeah," Healy said, "you do that."

Trask said, "Got any theories, Lieutenant?"

"I'd guess someone was in here expecting no one to be home, and Maguire came in and surprised him. There was a fight, Maguire went for the poker, and whoever it was hit him with something else and broke his neck. Then he got out of here."

"From the way the rug's bunched up and the body's lying, I figure he came at him from the dining room," I said.

Healy said, "Maybe."

Trask said, "How'd he get in?"

"That's a problem. Maybe one of the screens was unlocked or the door was ajar. Maybe somebody had a key."

Trask looked shocked. "Wait a minute, who the hell would have a key except the family?"

Healy shrugged. "Maybe the lock was picked," Trask said.

"How long you been chief here?" Healy asked.

"Seven years," Trask said. "Before that I was a sergeant."

"How many people have you run into out here that can pick that kind of a lock?" I said.

"There's always a first time."

"We'll wait and see what the dotor can give us," Healy said. "If I was you, Trask, I'd put a man here."

"I had one, but when Mrs. Bartlett went off with Spenser,

I took him off. She was supposed to call when she came back. I only got twelve goddamned men, Healy."

"I know. Spenser, you hanging in here?"

"Yeah. I'm staying in the guest room. If you get a chance, let me know what the doctor says about cause of death."

"Oh, of course," Healy said. "Want I should iron your shirts for you or anything while I'm here?"

I let that pass. "Well," I said, "time to dig out the old gold lamé tux and freshen up for the party."

Both Trask and Healy looked very sourly at me. I knew how they felt. I felt the same way.

15

Helping Margery Bartlett overcome her grief involved a lot of housework. The caterer arrived about twenty minutes after they'd hauled Maguire away in a blanket. He had two eight-foot tables in his truck and enough food to cover both of them. It was warm and I had my coat off. The caterer's assistant stared covertly at the gun on my hip but made no comment. I helped them set up the tables and carry in the food.

Marge Bartlett was hustling about in a passion of haste, directing me where to put the cold ham and what kind of silverware needed to go beside the schmaltz herring. Roger Bartlett got home about six o'clock and was told to set up the bar before he was told about Earl Maguire.

"Sonova bitch," he said, "sonova bitch." He kept shaking his head as he lined the bottles up on the counter in the kitchen. At six thirty Marge Bartlett retired to her room to begin getting ready, and Roger Bartlett went down to the store for soda. I called Susan Silverman. It was late on a Saturday, but there was no harm trying, and if I had to stand around at a cocktail party in the subs, I might as well have a date. She answered on the second ring.

"Mrs. Silverman, I'm calling to tell you that you've won the Jackie Susann look-alike contest. First prize is an

120

evening with a sophisticated sleuth at the Bartletts' cocktail party tonight."

"And second prize is two evenings," she said.

"Well, I'm doing guard duty here, and I wondered if you wanted to come along and carry my ammo."

"Seriously?"

"Seriously."

"Okay. What is anyone wearing?"

"I would say it's dress-up stuff. You know, sixty-five people. The food catered. A punch bowl. Ice sculpture. White linen tablecloth. Real silver. Mrs. Bartlett has started getting ready, and the guests don't come till eight."

"All right, I'll dress accordingly. Will you pick me up?"

"No, I'm sorry, I can't. There was a murder here today and Mrs. Bartlett's been threatened and I can't leave her. Can you drive yourself over okay?"

"A murder? Who?"

"The Bartletts' lawyer, Earl Maguire. I'll tell you about it tonight."

"What time do I arrive?"

"Eight o'clock."

"See you then."

I said good-bye. There was a pause at the other end, then she said, "Jackie Susann?"

"Maybe it was Jackie O.," I said.

She said, "Well, it's better than Jackie Coogan, I suppose," and hung up.

Bartlett came back in the house with a case of club soda and put it on the floor beside the refrigerator.

"I'm going to take a shower," I told him. "Lock the door and don't let anyone in till I'm back down here. Okay?" I was much jumpier about the threats to Marge Bartlett since Maguire had turned up dead.

"Well, don't be long," he said. "I gotta get ready too."

"Ten minutes," I said.

"Right."

"Oh, by the way, I've invited a woman I know, Mrs. Silverman from the high school. I hope you don't mind."

"Mind? Hell no. A man needs some female companionship, long as he doesn't get carried away and end up married. You know? Don't need to be married to have fun. Right? Don't need that."

"Sure don't," I said, heading up the stairs.

I stuck to my word and was out of the shower in four minutes and dressed in another five. I put on a dark blue two-button suit with wide lapels and a shaped waist, a blue and white checked shirt, and a wide red tie striped blue and black. I didn't have any shoe polish, but I managed to freshen up my black boots with some Kleenex. I clipped my gun on and went back downstairs. I hoped there'd be no gunplay tonight. My hip holster was brown, and it didn't go with my outfit.

At eight the first guests began to arrive. Marge Bartlett was still getting ready, but her husband was there at the door dressed fit to kill. He had on a green and gold paisley-print jacket that was loose-fitting around the collar, a yellow shirt with long collar points, a narrow green and red paisley tie, brown flared slacks with cuffs, and black and brown blunt-toed stacked-heel shoes which made him walk a little awkwardly. His tailor looked to be Robert of Hall. How he must have yearned for a blue work shirt and khaki pants.

I stood around the hall with a can of beer in my hand as Bartlett let the guests in. He kept saying "Say hello to old Spenser here; he's a detective," which produced a lot of warm handshakes. I felt like a weed at a flower show.

Susan Silverman showed up at eight thirty, and a lot of people, mostly but not exclusively men, turned and looked at her. She was wearing a full-length backless dress with red and black flowers against a white background. The top tied in two thin strings around her neck. Her arms and back were still tanned from summer, and her black hair glistened. She had red earrings and fingernails to match. I introduced her to Bartlett.

"Hey," he said, "aren't you down the high school?"

"Yes, I'm a guidance counselor."

"Boy, they didn't look like you when I was in high school. Hey, Spenser? I bet they didn't look like that in your high school, huh?"

"No," I said, "nothing like that."

Marge Bartlett appeared. She was carrying a dark scotch and water in one hand and seemed the ultimate triumph of Elizabeth Arden. No hint of flesh showed through the uninterrupted gleam of her makeup. She wore a violet lavender top with long puffy sleeves and a deep neckline that showed a lot of cleavage. The kind of cleavage that required artifice. There were false eyelashes and pale lipstick and lavender nail polish the color of the eye shadow. Her lower half was covered in black crepe that dragged on the floor. I could never tell if it was a skirt or pants, and I forgot to ask Susan. Small black beads, maybe obsidian, hung in several coils from her neck, and black and lavender earrings swayed like exotic fruit from her ears. Her lavender shoes were open-toed with very high black heels. Her toenails were painted the same color as her fingernails.

Everything fitted very snugly, and one got a sense of Latex stretched, of pressures tightly contained. Her bright blond hair was artfully tousled over her forehead and doubtless sprayed in place. She embraced one of the men, a short, fat guy with a long crew cut and a guardsman mustache, holding her head back so's not to mess her hair and turning away as he tried to kiss her so's not to mess the makeup.

"Vaughn, you gorgeous hunk," she cried, "if your wife weren't such a good friend of mine—"

Two more couples arrived, and she turned toward them, leaving Vaughn with his mouth half-open. The wives, one tall and handsome with early gray salting her black hair, the other small, blond, and pretty, stopped to talk with Marge Bartlett; the husbands headed directly for the buffet spread in the dining room. I watched them go. One was middle height and muscular with rounded shoulders and the kind of rolling walk associated normally with sailors and gorillas. His buddy was shorter and wider with the body of a Turkish wrestler and the haircut of a monk.

"Beer," I said to Susan. "And I'll bet they never leave the buffet."

"The taller one's the hockey coach at the high school," she said.

"How about the other guy?"

"I don't know him; maybe he's a violinist."

"Yeah," I said, "or an elephant tamer."

Marge Bartlett moved into the living room, where the noise and smoke were already thickening. I said to Susan, "Come on. Whither she goest you and I goest as well. Or at least I do."

"Whither thou goest . . ." she said.

"How about whither I liest?" I said.

"I'm going to get us a drink. You want one?"

"Beer," I said. "I'm sorry it's self-service, but I'm working."

"I know."

She left me and returned shortly with a can of beer and a scotch on the rocks. She gave me the beer. Marge Bartlett had settled herself carefully on one arm of the living room sofa, not far from where Earl Maguire had gotten his neck broken. She was talking with three businessy-looking guys and inhaling her wine-dark scotch and water.

"What happened here today?" Susan Silverman asked. We stood in the archway that separated the living room from the front hall, and she rested one hand lightly on my upper arm. I restrained the urge to flex it.

"Somebody hit a lawyer named Earl Maguire on the side of the head so hard it broke his neck and he died. Or that's probably what happened. I found him here dead with his neck broken and a large bruise on the side of his face."

"Do you have any idea who?"

"Nope, nor why. There had been a threatening phone call directed at Mrs. Bartlett which seemed as bizarre and disjointed as everything else going on here. That's why I'm doing my centurion routine."

"And she's going on with the party just like this?" Susan shook her head. "I don't know if that's courage or obsession or madness."

"I don't either," I said, "but courage doesn't seem the most likely choice."

A middle-sized handsome man stopped in front of us. "A real blast, huh?" he said.

"Yeah," I said, "Fake ones are better than none, though."

"You bet your ass," he said. He slurred the *s*'s, and I realized he was drunk already. "Marge and Rog really know how to throw a blast. What you do?"

"I'm a grape stomper at a winery. I stopped by here to get my feet bleached."

Susan Silverman giggled at my elbow. I said, "It's an old George Gobel line." The handsome man said, "I'm into confidence training myself. If you believe in your product, then, by God, you can sell it, ya know? And the greatest product ya got to sell is yourself. Right?"

"I don't know," I said. "I'm not sure I'm for sale."

"Oh, yeah. Look, you wouldn't believe the change a confidence seminar can make in your whole approach to living. I mean, it's like getting psyched up for a football game, ya know? I'm going all over the state having these confidence seminars, and the results are fantastic, fan-tas-tic."

"How about not giving one right now though; my ears are beginning to smart."

"You got some terrific sense of humor. What did you say your name was?"

"Spenser."

"Well, Spence, you got some terrific sense of humor. I like that. This the little woman?"

Susan Silverman looked as if she were carsick.

He went on, "I was into losing, ya know? And so I took this confidence seminar and they showed me how I wasn't using all my potential and now I'm part of the team and running the seminars myself. What'd you say you did?"

"I said I was a grape crusher at a winery, but I was only kidding."

"Yeah, I got that. What's your real job? I mean, maybe I could help you or your people, ya know? Maybe you could use a little confidence."

Susan Silverman said, "Do you have a program for overconfidence?"

He frowned. "No. But you know, there might be a market there. You got a pretty good head for business for a lady. By God, I never thought of that." He moved off.

Marge Bartlett said something to one of the businessy types and stood up. He gave her a slap on the rear end, and all three men on the couch laughed. Marge Bartlett moved away and headed for the kitchen. I moved along after her.

Susan said, "I'll be along. I think I'll sample the buffet before those two guys finish it."

As I passed the dining room, I noticed the coach and his buddy still at the buffet. A colony of beer cans had sprung up on the highboy beside them. In the kitchen Roger Bartlett was mixing drinks at the counter from half-gallons of booze. A plastic trash can was filled with chopped ice and beer cans, and a whole ham garnished with fruit was being readied for the buffet table. I wondered if the two gourmets in the corner had already polished off the first one. It would be fun to join them and comment on the broads and make wisecracks about the other guests and eat and drink till it became self-destructive and have your wife drive home. That would be more fun than finding a guy with his neck snapped, or going one-on-one with a weight lifter. Or following Marge Bartlett around all evening. I looked around for Mr. Confidence. I needed a booster shot.

Bartlett poured a glass near full of sctoch, added an ice cube and a teardrop's worth of water, and gave it to his wife. She took a big drink and said, "Whoooo, that's strong. You want me to get drunk so you can take advantage of me."

"Dear, by the time I get to the bedroom tonight, you'll be snoring like a hog."

"Roger!" she said and turned away. She saw me standing in the doorway and came over.

"My God, Spenser, you're a big handsome brute," she said and leaned against me with her right arm around me.

I said, "You're really into words, aren't you?"

"He's my bodyguard," Marge Bartlett said to a woman with bags under her eyes and a pouty mouth. "Don't you think I ought to keep my body very close to him so he can guard it?" She made snuggling motions at me. Pressed against me, she felt tightly cased and ready to burst, like a knockwurst.

The woman with the baggy eyes said, "Someone should guard your body, sweetie, that's for sure."

I said, "You're leaning on my gun arm."

She put her mouth up close to my ear and said, "I could lean on something else, if you were nice."

"It wouldn't carry the weight," I said.

"You're awful," she said and stepped away from me.

I said, "All us big handsome brutes are like that."

Baggy-eyes snickered, and Marge Bartlett spotted Mr. Confidence across the kitchen and went after him.

"Are you really a bodyguard?" Baggy-eyes said.

"Yep."

"Do you have a gun?"

"No," I said. "I have this mysterious power I acquired in the Orient to cloud men's minds so they cannot see me."

Susan appeared with an assorted platter from the buffet table and offered me some. "I have two forks," she said. Baggy-eyes moved off. Marge Bartlett and Mr. Confidence were in close proximity across the kitchen. I wondered if she had called him a big handsome brute.

"Having a nice time?" Susan asked.

"It's better than getting bitten by a great white shark," I said.

"Oh, it's not that bad. In fact, you kind of like it. I've been watching you. You look at everything; you listen to everybody. I bet you know what everyone in the kitchen is talking about and what they look like. They fascinate you."

"Yeah," I said, "I'm into people."

"Oh, you're such a big tough guy, and you think you're funny, but I'll bet if that fool with the confidence courses got in trouble, you'd get him out of it."

"A catcher in the rye," I said.

"You're being smart, I know, but that's right. That's exactly what you are. You are exactly that sentimental."

The wall phone in the kitchen rang. A thin woman said, "Oh, Christ, that's my kid, I'll bet anything." And a tall white-haired man with a red face and a green polka-dot bow tie answered. "Duffy's Tavern, Archie the manager speaking." He listened and then he said, "Anybody here named Spenser?" The thin woman said, "Whew." I took the phone and said hello.

"Mr. Spenser? This is Mary Riordan at the State Police. Lieutenant Healy asked me to call you and tell you that Earl Maguire died of a broken neck apparently the result of being struck on the side of the face with a solid blunt object."

"Son of a gun," I said. "Thank you."

She hung up. Susan looked at me and raised her eyebrows.

"Nothing," I said. "Just a confirmation on the cause of death. I asked Healy to let me know, and he did. I didn't think he would."

"Who's Healy?" she asked.

"State cop."

I looked across the kitchen and was suddenly aware that I didn't know where Marge Bartlett was. "Where'd Marge Bartlett go?" I said to Susan.

"I don't know. Just a minute ago she was over there talking to a fat guy with a mustache."

I walked through the kitchen to the dining room. And on into the living room. No sign. I felt the first small tug of anxiety in my stomach. Atta boy, lose your goddamned assignment in her own house. On either side of the fireplace in the living room were French doors, thinly curtained. One was slightly ajar, and I walked toward it. Outside I heard someone say in a half scream, "Don't, don't." The little tug in my solar plexus darted up to my throat, and I jumped through the door. I was on a screened porch that ran the whole side of the house. In the dim light I could see a man and a woman struggling. The man had his back to me, but I could see the woman's face across his shoulder, white in the dimness. It was Marge Bartlett. She wrenched away from him as I came onto the porch. I took one step with my left foot, planted it, turned sideways, and drove my right foot into the small of the man's back. He said, "Ungh," and went headfirst through the screen and into a mass of forsythia. I went after him. Marge Bartlett was screaming. The man was sluggishly trying to get out of the forsythia. I got his right arm bent up behind him and my left hand clamped under his chin and dragged him back on the porch.

He was protesting, but not coherently. The porch light snapped on. People were crowding out on the porch. The guy I had hold of was Vaughn, the fat man with the crew cut and the big mustache who had been one of the first to arrive.

"Goddamned tease," he was yelling now. "She got me out here; I didn't do anything. Goddamned stinking tease. Get you hot and then scream when you touch her. Bastard. Bitch." There were scratches on his face where he went through the screen. There was lipstick on his face too. I looked at Marge Bartlett; her lipstick was smudged. The deep V-neck of her blouse was torn, and some of a black longline bra showed.

"Let him go, Spenser. Are you crazy? We were just talking. For God's sake, haven't you ever been to a party? We were just talking, and I guess he got the wrong idea. You know how men are." Dimly visible through her makeup her face seemed to be red. "They always get the wrong idea. I was just surprised. I could have handled this. Look at my screen. Look . . ." I let the man go.

"Goddamned liar. You got me out here and started playing goddamned kissy-face with me and rubbing your boobs up against me and when I get serious you start screaming and yelling and your goddamned gorilla comes charging out and hits me from behind."

"Gorilla?" I said.

Susan Silverman had come up beside me. "*Goddamned gorilla*," she said.

16

It was two thirty-five in the morning. The noise was dense and tangible in the living room. Marge Bartlett had changed from a lavender to a yellow top, and the lavender trimmings she still wore glared more brusquely than ever. Vaughn, his back sore but unbroken, had collected his very silent and thin-mouthed wife and departed. The stereo was playing, and Billie Holiday's remarkable voice cut through the coarse air. "*. . . Papa may have, but God bless the child that's got his own . . .*" I edged a little closer so I could listen.

Two women, one red-haired, one brunette, both wearing pants suits a little tighter than they should be, were talking between me and the speakers.

"Do you think she'll pass out?"

"Why should this party be different?"

"She's got to be drunk out of her mind to be wearing that top with those earrings. She'd never do that sober. One thing you can always say for Margie, her taste in clothes is terrific."

"It's a little wild for her age."

Across the room Susan was talking with a tall, thin dark-faced man with flaring nostrils that gave him the look of an Arabian horse. It was Dr. Croft. His hair was short and slicked straight back. His sideburns, thin and barbered, came to his jawline. He patted her hip. I squeezed past the fashion commentary and came up beside Susan and put my hand on her shoulder.

"Oh, Spenser," she said, "I'd like you to meet Doctor Croft."

I said, "We met briefly. How are you, Doctor Croft?"

He smiled and put out his hand. "Ray," he said. "Good to see you again."

We shook hands. His fingers were very long and showed the marks of a manicurist. They thickened at the ends.

"What's your specialty?" I asked.

"General practice." Again the big brilliant smile. When he smiled, the lines around his mouth became very pronounced. "I'm a specialist in general practice. It's what medicine is about, I believe. People to people. Is Mrs. Silverman here with you?"

"Yes." I phrased a remark about hip touchers but thought it would be immature to make it. So I didn't.

"I understand you're a detective."

"Yes."

"I understand you kicked Vaughn Meadows through a screen a little while ago." His wide mouth was almost lipless, and when he smiled he looked less like an Arabian horse and more like a shark.

"Mistaken identity," I said.

"That's okay," he said. "Vaughn Meadows would be a far better person if someone would give him a kick in the ass about weekly." His smile shut off, and a serious frown replaced it. "It's a terrible sequence of things that has befallen this family."

I nodded. Susan said, "Isn't it? The Bartletts seem so resilient, though. They keep bearing up."

"How about the boy?" Croft asked. "Is there any trace of him?"

I shook my head. "Haven't been able to look for him lately. I've had to stick around his mom."

Croft rattled the ice cubes in his glass. "Looks like I'm empty," he said. "Excuse me while I fix myself a new one. Getting through one of these parties sober is more than I could do." He bared his brilliant shark smile again and then closed it off like a trap shutting and went to the kitchen.

"He appeared to be patting you on the hip," I said.

"That's why you came over." Susan smiled and shook her head. "Were you prepared to defend my virtue?"

"I'm in pursuit of it myself, and I don't like poachers."

"He's a very big man in this town," Susan said. "Board of Selectmen, Conservation Commission, adviser to the Board of Health, used to be Planning Board chairman. All the best people have him when they're sick."

"He's a hip patter," I said.

"Very wealthy," she said. "Very big house."

"Pushy bastard," I said.

"I wonder what it is in women," she said. "Whenever they find a big strong guy with a wide adolescent streak running through him, they get a powerful urge to hold his head in their laps."

"Right here?" I said.

"About now I think we could probably marry and raise a family here without anyone noticing."

She was right. It looked like a Busby Berkeley production of Dante's *Inferno*. To my left in the dining room the food was scattered on the table and floor. The platters were nearly empty, and the tablecloth was stained and littered with potato salad, cole slaw, miniature meatballs, tomato sauce, mustard, ham scraps, ring tabs, ashes, and things unrecognizable. The detritus of jollity.

The hockey coach had departed, but his buddy remained, red-eyed and nearly motionless, in his oversized right hand a can of beer, and a platoon, perhaps a company, of its dead companions in silent formation on the highboy beside him. His wife was speaking sharply to him with no effect.

Marge Bartlett was back on the couch between two of the business types in the razor-styled haircuts and the double knit suits. She was talking thickly, her mouth loose and wet, an iceless drink in her right hand, her left rubbing the thigh of one of the men. As she talked, the two men exchanged grins behind her head, and one of them rolled his eyes upward and stuck his tongue out of the left corner of his mouth.

"I'm a very nice person," she was saying. It came out "nishe pershon."

"Hey Marge," one of the business types said, "you know the definition of a nice girl?"

"One who puts it in for you," I murmured to Susan.

"I know," she said. "It's a very old joke."

"One that puts it in for you," the business type answered his own question, and both men laughed very loudly.

Marge Bartlett looked puzzled, a look I'd seen before. She took a slug from her glass.

Roger Bartlett had gone to bed. The good-looking guy who ran confidence courses seemed to be running one in the oversized chair in the corner with a woman I hadn't seen before. There was a flash of bare thigh and lingerie as they moved about.

"Maybe I *will* take that guy's confidence seminar," I said to Susan.

She looked and glanced away quickly. "Jesus," she said, "I think I'm shocked."

"I guess you don't want to make reservations for the chair later on then?"

She shook her head. "That poor kid," she said. "No wonder he's gone."

"Kevin?"

She nodded.

"You think he ran away?"

"Wouldn't you," she said, "if you lived here?"

"I've been thinking about it," I said.

17

Marge Bartlett got to bed about four. I helped her up the stairs, and she stumbled into her bedroom in a kind of stupefied silence. The lights were on. Roger Bartlett was sleeping on his back with his mouth open. On the bureau a small color TV set flickered silently, the screen empty, a small barren buzz coming from it. Marge Bartlett moved painfully toward her twin bed. I closed the door, went to the guest room, undressed, and flopped on the bed. If I lived here, I might run away. The room was warm, and some of the smoke from downstairs had drifted up. But if the kid ran away, why the merry prankster kidnap gig? Why all that childish crap with the coffin? Maybe that was it. Childish. It was the kind of thing a kid would do. Why? "The little sonova bitch hates us," Marge Bartlett had said. But Maguire, that wasn't the kind of thing a kid would do. Or could do. Somebody had hit Maguire very hard. Where would the kid go if he ran away? Harroway's place? He had something for Harroway, obviously. Harroway could hit somebody very hard. I fell asleep.

When I woke up it was ten o'clock. No one else was up. I stood for a long time under the shower before I got dressed. Downstairs looked like the rape of Nanking. Everywhere there was the smell of stale cigarettes and booze and

degenerating shrimp salad. Punkin appeared very pleased to
see me and capered around my legs as I let him out the back
door. The Smithfield police cruiser was parked in the
driveway again. Ever vigilant. I found an electric percolator
and made coffee. I brought a cup out to the cop in the
driveway.

I hadn't seen him before. He had freckles and looked
about twenty-one. He was glad to get the coffee.

"You going to be here all day?" I asked.

"I'm on till three this afternoon, then someone else
comes on."

"Okay. I'm going to be gone for a while, so stay close. If
they're looking for me, tell them I'm working. Don't let her
go out alone, either."

"If I have to take a leak, is it okay if I close the door?"

"Why don't you wait till you're off duty," I said.

"Why don't you go screw an onion," he said.

There seemed little to say to that, so I moved off. The
morning was glorious, or maybe it just seemed so in
contrast to the situation indoors. The sky was a high bright
blue with no clouds. The sun was bright, and the leaves had
begun to turn. Some of the sugar maples scattered along
Lowell Street were bright red already. There weren't many
cars out. Church or hangover, I thought. I found the turn for
Harroway's house, drove about a hundred yards beyond it,
and pulled off on the side of the road.

If my mental map was right, I could cut across the woods
and get a look at the house and grounds from a hill to the
right of the road we'd driven in. It had been awhile since I
took a walk in the woods, and the sense of it, alone and
permanent, was strong as I moved through the fallen leaves
as quietly as I could. I was dressed for stalking: Adidas
sneakers, Levi's jeans, a black turtleneck sweater, blue

nylon warm-up jacket, thirty-eight caliber Smith and Wesson. Kit Carson.

A swarm of starlings rose before me and swooped off to another part of the woods. Two sparrows chased a blue jay from a tree. High up a 747 heaved up toward California, drowning out the protests of the jay. There was low growth of white pine beneath the higher elms and maples, and thick tangles of thorny vines growing over a carpet of leaf mold that must have been two feet thick.

The land rose slowly but steadily enough so that I began to feel it in the tops of my thighs as I reached the crest. The hill down was considerably steeper, and the house was below in a kind of punch-bowl valley, a shabby building in a cleared patch of gravel and weeds among the encroaching trees.

The engine noise had been a generator. I could see it from here. There were five-gallon gasoline cans clustered around it, but it was silent at the moment. Conserving energy? Out of gas? A late model two-toned pink and gray Dodge Charger was parked, sleek and incongruous, behind the house. I looked at my watch. Twelve minutes past ten in the morning. Probably sleeping late out here on nature's bosom. I sat down and leaned against the base of a maple tree and watched. In the next two hours six more planes flew over. Then about twelve fifteen the young girl I'd seen before came out with a big cardboard box, jammed it into a rusty perforated barrel, and set it ablaze. She had on, as far as I could tell, exactly what she'd been wearing before. White too-big T-shirt, wide-flared jeans, no shoes. Maybe she had ten outfits all the same. She paused to light a cigarette from the blaze and then went back inside. At twelve thirty the mongrel bitch came out and nosed around near the burning trash till she found a scrap of bone that hadn't made it to the incinerator. She rolled on it several times, then took it to the corner of the house and buried it.

At one twenty-two Kevin Bartlett came out of the house with Vic Harroway. The boy's arm was around Harroway's waist and Harroway's arm was around the boy's shoulder. Like lovers. They walked to the Charger, separated. The boy got in the passenger's side, Harroway got in the driver's side, and they drove away. Just like that. They drove away, and I sat on my butt under the maple tree and watched them. We never sleep. We just sit and watch.

I sat and watched for the rest of the day and into the night. They didn't come back. I was beginning to hallucinate about cheeseburgers and cashew nuts by the time I gave up. It was after eleven when I headed back through the woods, stumbling more in the dark. Visions of pepper steaks danced in my head. When I got really hungry, I never thought about coq au vin or steak Diane. I wondered why that was, but I had trouble concentrating because I kept thinking about the American chop suey my mother used to make and how I felt after I had eaten it. It was a lot better than thinking how I'd found Kevin Bartlett and lost him in the space of say, fifteen seconds. By the time I got to my car, I had a long scratch across the back of one hand from the thorny vines, and one eye was tearing from a twig. That time of night is cold in September north of Boston, and I turned on the heater. I found a place to eat that advertised itself as a "pub." I think I was the only person there to eat. I jammed in at a stool at the bar and ordered three hamburgers and a beer. The beer came in a big stein that must have held half a quart. I drank two before the hamburgers arrived with two slices of kosher dill pickle and a handful of potato chips on an oval platter. It was a little hard to distinguish the hamburg from the bun, but I didn't mind; I was busy trying not to break into a sweat as I ate. The place was obviously a

singles spot or pickup bar. The sound system was up full
blast and featured high velocity hard rock music without
interruption. All the booths and tables were filled, with
people, mostly subthirty, standing together in between them
and moving but barely on a very small dance floor. It was
dim and very smoky. The décor was standard: dark panels,
red carpet, psuedobarn. I was jostled often as I ate, once
while drinking, and the beer dribbled down my chin and
soaked through my stalking sweater. A bartender in a red
Ike jacket and a mod blond haircut put a bowl of peanuts in
front of me and refilled my beer glass.

I sipped at it now that the beast within had been pacified.
At least I knew that Kevin's stay with Harroway was
voluntary. They liked each other. Maybe stronger. That was
apparent from the hillside. Almost like lovers. His parents
would be relieved at least that he was safe. But that didn't
do anything for explanation. Or maybe it did. Maybe it
made the explanation worse. Maybe Kevin was in on all
that stuff. Maybe he was in on the death threats. Maybe he
was in on Maguire's death. Good news and bad news, Mr.
and Mrs. Bartlett, your kid's not dead. He's a murderer.
Which is the good news you say? How the hell do I know?
If I knew that kind of stuff, would I be sitting alone in a
singles bar in a strange suburb at twelve thirty-five on a
Sunday night? I'm a detective; I just find out things. I don't
solve things. Well no, I don't know where your boy is right
this minute, ma'am. Yes, sir, they drove away while I was
up on the hill watching. I watched closely, though. Balls.
The next guy that jostled me while I was drinking beer I was
going to level. Trouble was the place was so crowded if I
swung at someone, I'd hit three people. I got up and shoved
my way out of the pub. I couldn't stand the thought of going
back to the Bartletts'. I drove on into Boston and went to
bed in my own apartment. I took the phone off the hook,
went right to sleep, and didn't dream.

18

I woke up about twenty minutes of ten within the bright tangible silence of my bedroom. I was glad to be there. I got up and went to the kitchen. The cleaning woman had been there yesterday, and the place gleamed. I squeezed a big glass of orange juice and drank it while I put the coffee on to perk. Then I took a shower and shaved very carefully. When I was through, the coffee was ready, and I drank a cup while I made breakfast. I took two egg rolls from the freezer and put them in the oven, sliced two pieces of Williamsburg ham, a thick slice from a wedge of Swiss cheese, added a paper-thin slice of red onion, and arranged them on a plate with some tomato quarters. When the egg rolls were heated, I split them and put them on the plate too. I put out a saucer of sour cream, then I poured a new cup of coffee and sat down on a stool at the counter to eat, and read the *Globe*.

It was eleven when I left the apartment, full of stomach and clear of eye. I drove over to the Harbor Health Club, the second floor of an old building on Atlantic Avenue. Until the new high-rise apartments had started going in along the waterfront, it had been the Harbor Gym, and once, when I'd thought I was a boxer, I'd trained there. I still went in sometimes to hit the speed bag and work on the heavy bag and maybe do some bench presses, but mostly I went to the

Y. The Harbor Gym had become upwardly mobile. Now it had steam rooms and inhalant rooms and exercise devices which jiggled your body while you leaned on them and chrome plating on the barbells and carpeting in the weight room.

I asked a receptionist in a toga where Henry Cimoli was, and she sent me to the Roman bath room. Henry was in there talking with two fat, hairy men who sat in a circular pool of hot water. Henry looked like an overdeveloped jockey. He was about five four in a snow-white T-shirt and maroon warm-up pants. The muscles in his arms bulged against the tight sleeve of the T-shirt, and his neck was thick and muscular with a prominent Adam's apple. There was scar tissue around his eyes. His thick black hair was cut close to his head and brushed forward.

"Spenser," he said when he saw me, "want a free go on the irons?"

"Not today, Henry. I want to talk."

"Sure." He spoke to the fat men in the hot water, "Excuse me, I gotta talk with this guy."

We walked back toward the cubbyhole office beyond the weight room.

"You still lifting?" Cimoli asked.

"Yeah," I said, "some. Too bad about how you're letting yourself go."

"Hey, I gotta work at it all the time. Guy my height, man, you let it go and you look like a fat broad in about two weeks."

"Yeah, after I go you better go sit in the tub with those two guys, get a real workout."

Cimoli shrugged. "Aw, you gotta offer that shit. They come in and sit in the steam room and soak in the pool and go home and tell everybody how they're getting in shape. But we got the real stuff too. You remember."

I nodded. "I'm looking for a guy, Henry." I showed him the picture of Vic Harroway. He took it and looked at it. "One of those guys, huh?" He shook his head. "Assholes," he said. I nodded again. Cimoli studied the picture. Then he broke into a big grin. "Yeah," he said. "Yeah, I know this bastard. That's Vic Harroway. I'll be goddamned, old Vicki Harroway, la *de* da."

"What do you mean, la *de* da?" I said.

"He's a fag. He's building himself up for the boys down the beach, you know?"

"Do you know that or do you just think it?"

"Well, hell, I mean he never made no pass at me, but everybody knows about Vicki. I mean, all the lifters know Vic, you know? He's queer as a square doughnut."

"He work out here?"

"Naw, he used to be the pro at a health club in one of the big hotels, but I heard he got canned for fooling around. I ain't heard of him in about a year or so."

"Any place he hangs out?"

Cimoli shook his head and shrugged. "Beats me," he said.

"Friends? People who knew him?"

"Christ, I don't know. I barely knew the guy. I seen him in a couple contests I had to judge—it's hokey, but it's good PR for the club—and you hear talk, but I don't know the guy myself. Why?"

"He's my weight-lifting idol. I want to find him so he can autograph this picture."

"Yeah, me too," Cimoli said. "Well, look, if I hear anything I'll give you a buzz, okay? Still in the same crummy dump?"

"I have not relocated my office," I said. "Better check the boys in the pool. Don't want them exhausting themselves first time out."

"Yeah, I better. They tend to get short of wind just climbing in."

When I got back out on the street, the bright day had turned dark. The city and the sky were the same shade of gray, and they seemed to merge so that there was no horizon. Vicki Harroway? Goddamn.

I drove back up onto the expressway, around Storrow Drive, off at Arlington Street, and parked in a tow zone by the Ritz a block from Boylston Street. The gray sky was spitting a little rain now, just enough to mist on my windows. Enough to make me turn the collar up on my sport coat as I headed up Newbury Street.

Halfway up the block, past the Ritz, on the same side was a five-story brick building with a windowed, five-story, pentagonal bay and a canopied entry. The bay window on the third floor said Race's Faces across it in black script outlined with gold.

I took the open-mesh black iron elevator up. It let me out right in the waiting room. Gold burlap wallpaper, gold love seat, gold glass-topped coffee table, gold wall-to-wall carpet, and a blond receptionist with centerfold boobs, in a lime-green chiffon dress, sitting at a lime-green plastic desk. On the walls were black and white photographs of women with lots of fancy-focus blurring and light glinting on their hair. To the right of the receptionist was a lime-green door with a black-lettered gold-trimmed script sign that said Studio.

The receptionist pointed her chest at me and said, "May I help you?"

"Yes, you may," I said, "but it would involve wrinkling your dress."

"Did you wish to make an appointment with Mr. Witherspoon, sir?"

"Doesn't he mind wrinkling his dress?"

She said, "I beg your pardon."

I said, "Never mind. I would, in fact, like to see Mr. Witherspoon."

"Did you have an appointment?"

"No, but if you'd tell him Spenser is here, I bet he'd see me."

"What is it you wish to see him about?"

"I'm posing for the centerfold in the December *Jack and Jill* and wondered if Race would be willing to handle the photography."

She picked up the phone and pressed the intercom button. "Mr. Witherspoon? I'm sorry to bother you, but there's a man here who says his name is Spenser. He said something about posing for some pictures in *Jack and Jill*. I'm not familiar with it. Yes sir." She hung up and said to me, "Mr. Witherspoon says to come in. He's right through that door."

"*Jack and Jill*," I said, "is a magazine that celebrates the heterosexual experience." She looked at me without expression and said, "Why don't you shove *Jack and Jill* magazine up your ass."

"Class will out," I said and went into the Studio.

It was white: floor, ceiling, walls, rugs, except one wall which was covered in uninterrupted black velvet. Opposite the door the room bellied out into the pentagonal bay I'd seen from the street. There were black velvet drapes gathered at each side of the windows. On a Victorian-looking black sofa a very thin girl reclined with her head propped on one elbow and a rose in her teeth. She was wearing a billowy diaphanous white gown, very red lipstick, and nail polish. Her black hair was very long and very straight. Surrounding her was a cluster of light poles and bounce lighting. Extension cords tangled around the floor near the sofa. Around her moved a graceful man with a Hasselblad camera.

Race Witherspoon was six feet tall, slim, tanned, and entirely bald. I never did know whether he was naturally bald or if he shaved his head. His eyebrows were black and symmetrical, and a blue shadow of closely shaved beard darkened his jaw and cheeks. He had on tight black velvet pants that rode low on his hips and tucked into white leather cowboy boots. His shirt was white silk, open almost to his belt. The sleeves were belled. His tanned chest was as tight-skinned and hairless as his head, and a big silver medallion hung on a silver chain against his sternum. Susan had an outfit like it. But Race's was more daring. He moved fluidly around the model with the Hasselblad, snapping pictures and cranking the film ahead.

"I'll be with you in a minute, old Spenser, my friend." He spoke while he shot. He wore a large onyx ring on his right index finger, and a black silk kerchief was knotted around his throat. Outside the bright bath of the photography lights, the room was dim, and the misting rain that had begun while I walked up Newbury Street had become a hard rain that rattled on the windows. I sat on the edge of an ebony free-form structure which I took to be a desk.

"All right, Denise, take a break while I talk to the man."

The model got up off the couch without any visible effort, like a snake leaving a rock, and slunk off through a door behind the velvet hangings on the far wall. Witherspoon walked over to me and put the camera down beside me on the desk.

"What is it I can do for you, Chickie?" he said.

"I've come for one last try, Race," I said. "I've got to know. What is your name, really?"

"Why do you doubt me?"

I shook my head. "No one is named Race Witherspoon."

"Someone is named anything."

I took out my photo of Vic Harroway and handed it to Witherspoon.

"I'd like to locate this guy, Race. Know him?"

"Hmm, fine-looking figure of a man. What makes you think I might know him?"

"I heard he was gay."

"Well, for crissake, Spenser, I don't know every queer in the country. It's one thing to come out of the damned closet. It's quite another to run a gay data bank."

"You know him, Race?"

"I've seen him about. What's your interest? Want me to fix you up; maybe you could go dancing at Nutting's on the Charles?"

"Naw, he'd want to lead. I think I'll just stay home and wash my hair and listen to my old Phil Brito albums. What do you know about Harroway?"

"Not much, but I want to know the rap on him before I say anything. I owe you some stuff, but, you know, I don't owe you everything I am."

"Yeah," I said. "You don't. Okay, there's a missing boy, about fifteen. I saw him with Harroway. I want the kid back, and I would like to ask Harroway about a murder."

Witherspoon's thick eyebrows raised evenly. "Heavy," he said. "Very heavy. A fifteen-year-old kid, huh? Harroway was always a damned baby-raper, anyway."

"He's got no record," I said.

"I know. I didn't mean literally. He's the kind of guy who likes young kids. If he were straight, he'd be queer for virgins, you know."

"He is gay, then?"

"Oh hell, yes."

"Where's he hang out?"

"I see him at a gay bar over in Bay Village, The Odds'

End. Isn't that precious? I don't go there much. It attracts a kinkier crowd than I like."

"Know what he does for a living?"

"No. I thought he lifted weights all the time. I know he was fired from a health club a year or so ago, and as far as I know he never got another job. He's around with a lot of bread, though. Fancy restaurants, clothes, new car. That kind of thing."

"Think he might kill someone?"

"He's a mean bitch, you know. He's a fag that doesn't like fags. He likes to shove people around. One of those I'm-gay-but-I'm-no-fairy types."

"Anything else you know that could help? Friends, lovers, anything?"

Witherspoon shook his head. "No, I don't know him all that well, only seen him around. He's not my type."

"Okay," I said. "Thank you."

"Now, on the other hand," Witherspoon said, "you are."

"Not with someone who won't give his real name," I said.

"Well, how about Denise then?"

"Not till you feed her," I said. "Your secretary, however, is another matter."

Witherspoon gave me a big smile. "Sorry, old Spenser, she's hot for Denise."

I said, "I think I'll go look for Harroway before I find myself mating with a floor lamp," and I left.

19

The Odds' End was on a side street off Broadway in the Bay Village section of Boston. The neighborhood was restored red-brick three-story town houses with neat front steps and an occasional pane of stained glass in the windows. The bar itself had a big fake lantern with Schlitz written on it hanging over the entrance and the name The Odds' End in nineteenth-century lettering across the big glass front.

I got a crumpled-up white poplin rain hat with a red and white band out of the glove compartment and put it on. I put on my sunglasses and tipped the rain hat forward over my eyes. Harroway had seen me only once, and then briefly; I didn't think he'd recognize me. I looked at myself in the rearview mirror and adjusted the hat down a little. Rakish. I turned up the collar on my tweed jacket. Irresistible. I got out of the car and went into The Odds' End.

It was dark inside, and it seemed darker with sunglasses. There was a bar along the left wall, tables in the middle, a jukebox, high-backed booths along the right wall, and an assortment of what looked like Aubrey Beardsley drawings framed above the booths and on either side of the jukebox.

A thin black man in pointed patent leather shoes and a green corduroy dungaree suit was nursing a brandy glass at the near end of the bar. His hair was patterned in dozens of small braids tight against his scalp. He looked at me as I came in, then went back to his brandy. On the bar in front of him was an open package of Eve cigarettes.

I sat at the far end of the bar, and the bartender moved down toward me. He was middle-sized and square with curly black hair cut close and a long strong nose. There were acne scars on his cheeks. He had on a blue oxford button-down shirt with the collar open and the cuffs rolled back. His hands were square and strong-looking. The nails were clean.

"Yes, sir," he said, looking at a point about two inches left of my face.

"Got draft beer?" I said.

"Miller's and Lowenbrau."

"Miller's is okay."

He put a cardboard coaster on the bar in front of me and a half-pint schooner on the coaster.

"I might be here awhile," I said. "Want to run a tab on me?"

"On the house," he said.

I widened my eyes and raised my eyebrows.

"I haven't seen you before, and I know most of the guys from Station Four. You from Vice?"

"Oh," I said, "that's why it's free."

"Sure, I spotted you the minute you walked in," he said.

Spenser, man of a thousand faces, master of disguise. "I'm not a cop," I said. "I just came in to kill a rainy afternoon. Honest."

The bartender put a tray of crackers and a crock of orange cheese in front of me.

"Yeah, sure, whatever you say, man," he said. "I'll run a tab on you if you want."

"Please," I said. "Actually, I'm kind of flattered that you thought I was a cop. Do I look tough to you?"

"Sure," he said, "tough," and moved down the bar to wait on a new customer. Maybe I should have worn my jade earrings.

The new customer probably wasn't a cop. He did have earrings. But they weren't jade. They were big gold rings. He was a middle-aged white man with gray hair pulled up into a topknot. He had on a red and gold figured dashiki that was too big for him and woven leather sandals. His fingernails were an inch beyond the ends of his fingers. He had come in at a sort of shuffling quickstep, his head still, his eyes looking left and right, like a kid about to soap a window. He was at the bar about halfway between the black guy at one end and me at the other.

"I'll have a glass of port, Tom," he said to the bartender in a soft raspy mumble.

"Got the bread, Ahmed?"

Ahmed reached inside the dashiki and came out with a handful of silver. It clattered loudly on the bar.

The bartender put a pony of wine on the bar in front of him and slid ninety cents out of the small pile of change. Ahmed chugalugged it and put the glass down on the bar. Tom filled it again, took the rest of the change, and moved away. Ahmed nursed the second one. He looked from me to the black guy in the green corduroy. Then he moved down near me.

"Hi," he whispered. He sounded like Rod McKuen doing the Godfather.

"Where'd you leave your spear?" I said.

"My spear?"

Close up Ahmed smelled stale, and the long fingernails were dirty.

"My, you're a big one," he said. "What's your name?"

"Bulldog Turner," I said.

"Hey, that's kind of a cute name, Bulldog." He squeezed my left bicep. "I bet you're awfully strong."

The bartender stood polishing shot glasses, watching us with no expression of any kind.

"But oh so gentle," I said.

"You gotta quarter for the jukebox?" He was rubbing his flat hand up and down the back of my arm. Close up there was a gray stubble of beard showing, maybe two days' worth. I gave him a quarter. "I'll be right back," he said and scuttled across to the jukebox. He played an old Platters record, "My Prayer," and hurried back to his stool beside me. He never straightened fully up. There was a hunched quality to him, like a dog that's just wet on the rug. He drank the rest of his wine.

"Wanna buy me a drink?" he asked. His breath was sour.

"Ahmed," I said, "I'll buy you two drinks if you'll take them down the other end of the bar. I think you're a fantastic looker, but I'm spoken for."

Ahmed hissed at me, "Mother sucker," and scooted down the bar.

I motioned the bartender. "Give him two drinks, on me," I said.

20

It was five more draft beers and two passes later that Harroway showed. It was about four thirty now, and The Odds' End had filled up. The jukebox was playing "Boogie-Woogie Bugle Boy of Company B," and two guys were doing the Funky Chicken in a small open area in front of it.

Harroway came in shrugging his shoulders to shake off the rain. He had an Aussie campaign hat on over his blond hair—probably didn't want the color to run—and a rust-colored wraparound leather overcoat with black epaulets, a black belt, and black trim at the collar, cuffs, and along the skirt. Slick. He scanned the bar while he took off the coat. His eyes ran over me with no hesitation and kept going. He hung the coat and hat on a rack at one of the booths and sat down. His back to me. I noticed his white shirt was a see-through model. Be still my heart.

The guy he sat down with was a fat Oriental-looking Italian man in a blue chesterfield overcoat with velvet lapels. He kept the coat buttoned up to the neck. The bartender came out from behind the bar and put two highball glasses down on their table and went back behind the bar. When he got back I paid my bill.

Harroway talked with the fat man for fifteen minutes,

finished his second drink, and stood up. He put on his leather coat and Aussie campaign hat, said something to the fat man, and went out into the rain, hunching his shoulders automatically as he opened the door.

I went after him. When I reached the street, he was already turning the corner toward Park Square. I hurried along, crossed to the other side of the street, and hung back about a half block behind him. It was raining hard and soaked through my tweed jacket in less than two blocks. Tailing a guy alone is mostly luck, and if he's being careful, it can't be done. Harroway, however, didn't seem worried about a tail. He never looked around. It was twenty past five on a Monday night, and the city was crowded with commuters. That made it easier. We crossed Park Square past the grateful statue of a freed slave. "Lawzy me, Marse Whitey, Ah'm pow'ful obliged fo' ma freedom." Balls.

We crossed Boylston and headed past the big United Fund sign up across the Common. The trees still had most of their leaves, and it cut the rain a little but not enough. We went up hill to the round bandstand. Harroway stopped there and looked around. I kept going with my head down and passed him. He ignored me and stood against the bandstand with his hands in his pockets, his collar up.

I went twenty yards further and stopped at a bench. I swayed a little, put one hand on the back of the bench, and stood half-bent-over as if I might be sick. Two old ladies with umbrellas went by. One of them said, "Sober up, sonny, and go home." With my head hanging like this, I could look back and see him standing in the dark; he hadn't moved. I eased myself onto the bench and lay down with my knees pulled up to my chest and my head resting on one arm. I could stare right at Harroway through the wet sunglasses. I hoped a cop didn't come by and run me off. On a night like this I had the feeling the cops were checking for crime down at the Hayes-Bickford cafeteria and making sure no one tried sneaking in the Park Street subway without paying.

It was cold and getting colder. The rain fell steadily on the exposed half of my face and got under my collar and ran down my neck. My gun was pressing into my hip, but since I was supposed to be passed out, I didn't dare shift to adjust it. A guy adjusting a holster looks like a guy adjusting a holster. I lay still and let the rain soak through my clothes.

Harroway shifted from one foot to the other, his hands jammed into the pockets of his leather coat, his campaign hat tilted forward over his face. Two sailors went by with a fat barelegged girl between them. One of the sailors said something I couldn't hear and slapped the girl on the fanny. Both sailors laughed. The girl said, "Oh, piss on you," and they went by. Ah, to be young and in love. Or even just upright and dry. A bum shuffled around the bandstand and spoke to Harroway. Harroway put one hand on the bum's shoulder, turning him around. Placed his foot against the bum's backside and shoved him sprawling into the mud. The bum picked himself up and shuffled away.

The cold rain had collected in my left ear. The whole left side of my face was beginning to feel glazed over, as if the rain were freezing. If something didn't happen pretty soon, I'd look like a gumshoe aspic. A lean man with a big black umbrella walked up past me from the direction of Tremont Street. He stopped beside Harroway. His right hand held the umbrella. In his left was a briefcase. I couldn't see his face, or even the upper half of his body, because he had the umbrella canted toward me against the drive of the rain. His lower half was in dark trousers and raincoat. He wore rubbers. A clandestine meeting in the rain and you wear your rubbers: Romance is dead. Harroway took out an envelope from inside his coat. The Umbrella Man handed him the briefcase and moved off down the hill away from me in his rubbers toward Charles Street. Harroway came past me toward Tremont carrying the briefcase. I had a very quick choice to make. I was pretty sure I could pick Harroway up again at The Odds' End or the ranch house. It looked as if Harroway had bought something covertly from the Umbrella Man. I wanted a look at him. I stumbled up off the bench and followed the black umbrella down the hill. I staggered legitimately now—my legs felt like two duckpins and my feet were numb. At the foot of the hill there was a lighted entry to the underground garage. The Umbrella Man stopped in front of it and closed the umbrella. It was Dr. Croft. He headed down the stairs to the garage. I didn't have a car there and saw no point in going too.

I turned back up the hill and ran as hard as I could back across the Common. I got to Tremont Street by the information booth with my chest heaving and sweat mixing with the rain on my face. No sign of Harroway. I turned right, down Tremont across Boylston. No sign of Harroway. I turned right on Stuart back toward The Odds' End. I passed my car. There was a soaked parking ticket under the wiper on the passenger side. I went into The Odds' End. No Harroway. I ordered a double cognac and sat at the bar to drink it. I think it saved my life. By the time I finished it, it was nearly midnight. Harroway hadn't returned. I had another cognac. My head felt a little light. I paid and headed out of the place. If I was going to pass out, I wanted it to be someplace where there wouldn't be mouth-to-mouth resuscitation. Driving back to my apartment, I tried to sort out what I'd bumped into today, but I was too cold and too tired and too wet. Images of steam rising from my shower stall kept getting in the way.

21

At ten thirty the next day, showered, shaved, warmed, and dried, with nine hours' sleep behind me and hot corn muffins nicely balancing cold vealwurst in my stomach, I headed back for Smithfield. I'd called my service before I left that morning and found that there were nine calls recorded from Marge Bartlett. I ignored them. I wanted Harroway and the kid. I didn't think Marge Bartlett was in all that much danger. I wanted the kid. At five after eleven I was parked along the side of the street just down from the corner of the road that led into Harroway's sylvan retreat. I didn't want to get left standing on a hill this time while they drove away. The road was the only way in or out. I'd settle in here. I watched for eight hours. Nobody went in. Nobody came out.

At seven fifteen Harroway's pink and gray Charger nosed out of the leafy road and turned right, away from me toward Smithfield. It was dusk, and I couldn't see if Kevin was in the car, but Harroway's big blond head was clear enough. I followed. We drove through Smithfield and straight up Lowell Street into Peabody to Route 1. On Route 1 we headed south back toward Smithfield. I drifted back a little on Route 1. Let two cars in between us so he wouldn't spot me. He pulled into the parking lot of a big new motel with an illuminated sign outside: Yes! We Have Water Beds! I pulled in after him and drove on past behind the motel, parked near the kitchen entrance, and hustled back toward the lobby. It was dark out now and bright inside. Harroway was at the desk apparently registering. A girl was with him. She was young, high school age. Her hair was blond and cut short and square. She was wearing harlequin glasses with blue rims and a high-necked white blouse with a small black bow tie. Ah, Dorothy Collins, I thought, where are you now?

The clerk pulled a key out of one of the mail boxes in back of the desk: first row, fifth from the left. He pointed down a corridor to the left of the desk, and the two of them went on down it, turned another left, and disappeared. I went in, got close enough to check the number on the box the key had come from—112—bought a newspaper at the cigar counter, and sat down behind it in a leather chair in the lobby. Now what? I could go knock on the door. "Hi, I'm Snooky Lamson. Is Dorothy Collins in there?" I was punchy from sitting and doing nothing for eight hours. Checking into a motel with a girl didn't seem to fit Harroway's reputation. At seven thirty in came the man who ran confidence courses.

"Mr. Victor's room, please," he said.

Holy Christ, I thought, something's happening. I might actually find out if I keep sitting long enough and don't run my mouth.

Mr. Confidence went the same way Harroway and escort had gone, and ten minutes later Harroway appeared. He went across the lobby and into the dining room. Got himself a table, ordered a drink, and looked at the menu. I went back to the cigar counter, bought two Baby Ruths, sat down again, and munched them behind my newspaper. By the time Harroway had finished his steak, I had read the

obituaries, the office equipment for sale classified, the ads
for Arizona real estate, and was going back to the funnies
for a second run-through on my favorite, "Broom Hilda."

Harroway had pie and two cups of coffee. I looked at my
watch—nine fifteen. We'd been there an hour and forty-five
minutes. I read "Broom Hilda" again. Harroway had a
brandy. At nine forty-five the girl came on down the
corridor and joined Harroway. He paid the bill, and they got
up and left. I let them. As soon as they were out the door, I
headed down the corridor toward Room 112. I figured the
Confidence Man would wait a bit before he left, and if I
could catch him there in the room, I might get a handle on
the case, or I might get a free introductory trial offer on a
confidence course. One never knows.

The door was locked. I knocked. There was no answer. I
knocked again, trying to get that Motel Manager sound in it,
firm but friendly. A voice said, "Who is it?" The voice was
not confident.

I said, "It's me, Vic."

The lock turned and the door opened a crack. I put my
shoulder into it, and in we went. He said, "Hey." I shut the
door behind me. The force of my charge made him back
into the bed and sit on it. He said, "What do you want?"
with absolutely no confidence at all.

I said, "Don't you remember me? We met at the
Bartletts' party."

He opened his mouth and closed it. He remembered.
"You're the detective," he said.

"Right, and I'm detecting at this very moment." He was
wearing jockey shorts and black socks. The bed he sat on
was rumpled. There were lipstick smears on the sheet. On
the dresser beside the color TV were two empty bottles of
Taylor pink champagne and two empty glasses, one with a

lipstick half moon on the rim. "You have just shacked up," I said. "And I have caught you."

"What are you talking about? You're crazy. You get out of my room right now."

"Aw, come on, sir. What is your name, by the way?"

"I'm not telling you. I don't have to tell you anything." His pants were draped over the back of a leatherette chair. I reached over and took his wallet out of the pocket. He said "Hey" again but stayed on the bed. I was out of his weight class anyway, but it is always hard to feel tough in your underwear. I found his driver's license: Fraser W. Robinson. I put the license back in the wallet and the wallet back in the pants.

"Now, Fraser, let us talk. I was sitting in the lobby when Harroway checked in with the jailbait. I was there when you came in and he came out. And I am here now. And I've got you. But I'll make a trade."

Fraser Robinson was looking at the door and at the window and at the four corners of the room, and nowhere did he see a way out.

"What kind of trade?"

"You tell me a lot of stuff about Harroway and the girl and the commune. And I tell no one anything about Harroway the girl and the commune and you. How's that for swaps?"

"What if I just call the manager and have you arrested for breaking into my room?"

"It's not your room. It's Mr. Victor's room. And I'd have to arrest you on suspicion of violating the Mann Act, possible statutory rape, contributing to the delinquency of a minor child, and resisting arrest. In fact, I think you'd probably get hurt resisting arrest."

"Look, if you want dough, I could get you some. I mean I haven't got much on me but..."

"Uh, uh," I said. "I want information." I took my gun out, flipped open the cylinder, checked the load, and flipped it shut. "You going to resist arrest," I said, "or are you going to tell me things?" I looked at him hard, as I'd seen Lee Marvin do in the movies.

"What do you want to know?" he said.

I put the gun back. "I want to know what Harroway is running over there. This setup was obviously arranged and obviously routine. Harroway's got a movable whorehouse going, and I want to know details and I want to know what else he has going."

"He's got everything else," Robinson said.

"Tell me."

"Drugs, dirty movies, sex shows, gang bangs, still photos, fetish stuff—you know, like if chains turn you on or leather bras and stuff."

"What kind of drugs?"

"I don't know. Everything, I guess. I'm not into drugs. I heard he didn't deal heroin. One of the girls was talking about Quads, but I don't really know."

"Where's he get the drugs?"

"I don't know. I told you I'm not into drugs."

"Yeah, that's right." I looked at the empty bottles. "You're into New York State champagne. I forgot. How did you get in touch with Harroway?"

"Doctor Croft. Gave me a little card with the phone number. Said if I was looking for anything, to call and say what I wanted."

"How'd he happen to do that?"

"I was having some trouble with my wife, you know. I mean she wasn't interested much in sex, and I thought maybe I was doing something wrong; you know, technique. So I went to Doctor Croft, and he said maybe I could find a release if I wanted to and it would make our marriage better and he gave me this card. Here, gimme my pants. It's still in my wallet." Robinson dug it out. A calling card cheaply printed with only a phone number.

Wise old Doc Croft. Save your marriage, son; get out and screw a groupie. "Your wife ever go to Doc Croft?" I said.

"No, why?"

"Never mind. Okay, what's the connection between Croft and Harroway?"

"I don't know. Neither one of them ever mentioned it. Croft never said another word about it after that time he gave me the card. I never brought it up to him. I mean, it's not the kind of thing you want to talk about, you know. I mean, how your wife is frigid and you have to go to others." He'd found the basis for his actions as he talked. It was all his wife's doing anyway, the bitch.

"How much does it cost?" I said.

"A hundred for a regular shack. That's all night, if you want, but I can't stay out all night. I mean, my wife won't even go to bed till I come home, you know? If you want something special, the price goes up from there."

The telling was building its own momentum, as if he'd had no one to tell about all this till now. He was getting excited. "Like sometimes I go for a nineteen-fifties' look, like little prim broads with high necks and wide skirts, sort of cute and high-class like, like ah, oh, you know, some of those broads on TV in the fifties, like . . ."

"Dorothy Collins," I said.

"Yeah, yeah, like her, and June Allyson in that movie about the ball player with one leg, like that. Well anyway. For a hundred and a half I get a chick like that, you know, dressed up and everything."

"Isn't that something," I said.

"And they'll cater parties too. You know, stag parties. Like I was at one down the Legion Hall one night they had five broads and a goat. And reefers for anyone that wanted them and a lot of other stuff I don't know about. Jesus, you should see the equipment on that goat."

"Sorry I missed it," I said. "Where's Harroway get the girls?"

"I don't know, but they're all young, and they live with him out somewhere on a farm or something. You know like Charles Manson, a commune or whatever. And I guess they'll do anything he says."

"Okay, Fraser," I said, "you're off the hook. But I know who you are and where you live and what your hobbies are. I'll keep in touch."

"Look, I told you whatever you wanted, right? I mean you got no reason to bring me into anything, have you? I mean if Harroway ever found out I told . . ."

"Mum's the word, Fraser. Put on your pants." I looked at the empty champagne bottles. "A hundred and a half," I said, "and you get domestic champagne." I went out and closed the door.

In the lobby I looked at my watch—ten fifteen; I was missing the Tuesday night movie again. Then it hit me. Tuesday night I was supposed to be having dinner with Susan Silverman, with maybe a surprise treat afterward. I was two hours and fifteen minutes late.

I called her from a pay phone. "Susan," I said, "I'm being held captive by the West Peabody Republican Women's Club which wishes to exploit me sexually. If I overpower my captors and escape, is it too late?"

There was silence. Then she said, "Almost," and hung up.

As I left the phone booth I saw Fraser Robinson walk out of the lobby and toward the parking lot. Five girls, I thought, and a goat? Jesus Christ.

22

I stopped to buy a bottle of Dom Perignon and still made it to Susan Silverman's by ten thirty-five. Susan let me in without comment. I held the wine out to her. "They were out of Annie Greenspring," I said.

She took it. "Thank you," she said. She had on a chocolate satin shirt with an oversized collar and copper-colored pants. "Do you want some now?"

"Yes."

"Then come out in the kitchen and open it. I have trouble with champagne corks."

The house was a small Cape with some Early American antiques around. A small dining room ran between the living room and the kitchen. There was a miniature harvest table set for two with white china and crystal wineglasses. Gulp!

The kitchen was walnut-paneled and rust-carpeted with a wagon wheel ceiling fixture hanging over a chopping-block table. She put the champagne on the table and got two glasses out of the cabinet. I twisted the cork out, poured, and handed her a glass.

"I'm sorry as hell, Susan," I said.

"Where were you?"

"Mostly sitting in the lobby at the Hideaway Inn reading 'Broom Hilda' and eating a Baby Ruth."

She picked up the champagne bottle and said, "Come on. We may as well sit by what's left of the fire." I followed her into the living room. She sat in a black Boston rocker with walnut arms, and I sat on the couch. There was a cheese ball and some rye crackers on the coffee table, and I sampled them. The cheese ball had pineapple and green pepper in it and chopped walnuts on the outside.

"This is even better than a Baby Ruth," I said.

"That's nice," she said.

I picked up the champagne bottle from where she'd set it on the coffee table. "Want some more?" I said. "No, thank you," she said. I poured some in my glass and leaned back. The fire hissed softly, and a log shifted with a little shower of sparks. The living room was papered in royal blue, with the woodwork white and a big print of *Guernica* over the fireplace.

"Look, Suze," I said. "I work funny hours. I get into places and onto things that I can't stop, and I can't call and I gotta be late. There's no way out of that, you know?"

"I know," she said. "I knew all the two and one half hours I was walking around here worrying about you and calling you a bastard."

"Is the dinner ruined?" I said.

"No, I made a cassoulet. It probably improves with age."

"That's good."

She was looking at me now, quite hard. "Spenser, what the hell happened to you? What were you doing?"

I told her. Halfway through she got up and poured herself some more champagne and refilled my glass. When I finished she said, "But where's Kevin?"

"I don't know. I figure that Harroway's got him stashed

somewhere else. In Boston, maybe. He must have gotten nervous after we were out to his house."

"And Harroway's running a whole, what, vice ring? Right here in town? How can he get away with it? I mean, this isn't a big town. How can the police not know?"

"Maybe they do know."

"You mean bribery?"

"Maybe, or maybe Harroway has friends in high places. Remember Doctor Croft was the one who shilled old Fraser Robinson onto Vicki's scam."

"But to corrupt the police . . ."

"Cops are public employees, like teachers and guidance counselors. They tend to give a community what it wants, not always what it should have. I mean, if you happen to go for an evening out with five broads and a goat, and you are a man of some influence, maybe the cops won't prevent it. Maybe they'll try to contain it and keep everybody happy."

The bottle of Dom Perignon was empty. Susan said, "I bought some too," and went to the kitchen to get it. I got another log out of the hammered-brass wood bucket on the hearth and settled it on top of the fire. Susan returned with the champagne. Mumm. Good. I was more than a domestic champagne date. Next time, she'd said. Tuesday, at my house. Hot-diggity. She sat down on the couch beside me and handed me the bottle. I twisted the cork out and poured.

"I always thought you had to pop it and make a mark in the ceiling and spill some on the rug," she said.

"That's for tourists," I said.

"Where are you now, Spenser? What do you make of everything?"

"Well, I know that Kevin is with Vic voluntarily. I know Vic is a homosexual."

"You don't *know* that."

"I haven't proved it, but I know it. I heard it from people I trust. I don't need to prove it."

"That's an advantage you have on the police, isn't it?"

"Yeah, one. Okay, so Harroway's gay and Kevin's staying with him. You told me that Kevin had unresolved sexual identity problems . . ."

"I said he might have . . ."

"Right, he might have sexual identity problems, so the relationship between them might be romantic. Agree?"

"Spenser, you can't just say things like that; there's so much more that goes into that kind of diagnosis. I'm not qualified . . ."

"I know, I'm hypothesizing. I don't have the luxury of waiting to be sure."

"I guess you don't, do you?"

"I figure Vic and Kevin are living together, and he finds in Harroway a combination of qualities he misses in his parents. I figure the kid ran off with Harroway and then afterward, out of hatred or perversity or boyish exuberance, they decided to put on the straights and make some money to boot. So they rigged the kidnapping, and they sent the notes and made the phone calls and shipped the guinea pig after it died. Then they went, maybe to get some things of Kevin's, maybe to steal the old man's booze, maybe to play a new trick, and broke into the house. Actually Kevin probably had a key. And Earl Maguire caught them and they panicked, or Harroway did, and he killed Maguire. You saw Harroway; you can imagine how he could hit someone too hard, and if he did he could make it permanent."

"But what do you suppose Doctor Croft has to do with all this?"

"Maybe nothing, maybe just doing a favor for his buddy, Fraser Robinson. Maybe he's no more than a satisfied customer. Or maybe he's a convenient source of drugs. An

M.D. has a better shot than most people at getting hold of narcotics. I can't see the mob doing business with the likes of Harroway."

"What are you going to do?"

"Well, I was thinking of putting my hand on your leg and quoting a few lines from Baudelaire."

"No, dummy, I mean what are you going to do about Vic Harroway and Doctor Croft and Kevin?"

"One thing I'll do right now. Where's your phone?"

"In the kitchen."

I got up and called Boston Homicide. "Lieutenant Quirk, please." Susan came out with me and looked at the cassoulet in the oven.

"Who's calling?"

"My name's Spenser."

"One moment." The line went dead and then a voice came on.

"Spenser, Frank Belson. Quirk's home asleep."

"I need a favor, Frank."

"Oh, good, me and the Lieutenant spent most of today hanging around thinking what could we do to be nice to you. And now you call. Hey, what a treat."

"I want to know anything you can find out about a medical doctor named Raymond Croft, present address . . ." I thumbed through the Smithfield phone book on the shelf below the phone, "Eighteen Crestview Road, Smithfield, Mass. Specializing in internal medicine. I don't know his previous address. Call me here when you can tell me something." I gave him Susan's number. "If I'm not here leave a message."

"You're sure you don't want me to hand-carry it out there?"

"Maybe I can do you a favor sometime, Frank."

"Oh, yeah, you could do everybody a favor sometime, Spenser."

The conversation wasn't going my way, so I let it go and hung up. "How's the cassoulet?" I said.

"On warm," she said. "It'll keep. I think we need more wine."

"Yes," I said, "I believe we do."

We went back into the living room and sat on the couch and drank some more. My head felt expanded, and I felt very clever and adorable.

"Darling," I said, leaning toward Susan, *"je vous aime beaucoup, je ne sais pas* what to do."

"Ah, Spenser, you romantic fool," she said and looked at me over the rim of her champagne glass while she drank. "Are you really a detective, or are you perhaps a poet after all?"

"Enough with the love talk," I said, "off with the clothes."

She put the champagne glass down and looked at me full face and said, "Be serious, now, please. Just for now." My throat got tight, and I swallowed audibly.

"I am serious," I said.

She smiled. "I know you are. It's funny, isn't it? Two sophisticated adult people who want to make love with each other, and we don't know how to make the transition to the bedroom. I haven't felt this awkward since college."

I said, "May I kiss you?" and my voice was hoarse.

She said, "Yes, but not here. We'll go in the bedroom."

I followed her down a short corridor and into her bedroom. There was a spool bed with a gold-patterned spread. An air conditioner hummed softly in the far window. The walls were covered in a beige burlap paper, and there was a pine sea chest at the foot of the bed.

She turned toward me and began to unbutton her blouse.

"Would you turn the spread down, please?" she said. I did. The sheets were gold with a pattern of coral flowers. As I undressed I looked at Susan Silverman on the other side of the bed. She unhooked her bra. There is something enormously female in that movement. I stopped with my shirt off and my belt unbuckled to watch her. She saw me and smiled at me and let the bra drop. I took a deep inhale and finished undressing. We were naked together then, on opposite sides of the bed. I could see the pulse in her throat. She lay down on her side of the bed and said, "Now you may kiss me."

I did. With my eyes closed, for a long time. Then I opened my eyes and discovered that she had hers open too and we were looking at each other from a half inch away. With her eyes wide open she darted her tongue into my mouth and then giggled, a rich bubbling half-smothered giggle that I caught. We lay there pressed together kissing and giggling with our eyes open. It was a different beginning, but a very good one. Then we closed our eyes again, and the giggling stopped.

23

We ate cassoulet and drank Beaujolais at two fifteen in the morning in the dining room with candles and didn't get to sleep till four. In the morning she called in sick, and we stayed in bed till almost noon. We had a cup of coffee together and cleaned up the dining room and kitchen. It was two o'clock in the afternoon before I was back to work.

Dr. Croft had an office in a medical building on one side of a small shopping center in the middle of Smithfield. Two stories, brick, pastel plywood panels, a flat roof, and maybe ten offices. Inside there was the cool smell of air-conditioned money. There were four people in Croft's office, three women and a man. Well, you see, Doctor, I'm horny but my spouse thinks I'm a creep. Oh, yes, of course, I'll make an appointment for you with Doctor Harroway, my horniness consultant.

The office was paneled in light plywood and carpeted in beige. A dark-faced girl with an enormous bouffant hairdo and a starched white uniform eyed me from behind a counter in the far wall. I said, "I'd like to see the doctor, please."

She said, "Have you an appointment?"

I said, "No, but if you'll give him my card and tell him it's important, I think he'll see me." I gave her a card with

172

just my name and address on it. The one with the crossed sabers on it might seem a little pushy, I thought.

"Have you ever been a patient of Doctor Croft's before?"

"No, ma'am."

"And what is your complaint?" She was pulling out a little yellow record card and rolling it into the typewriter.

"Functional curiosity about a guy named Fraser Robinson."

She stopped rolling the record form into the typewriter and looked at me. "I beg your pardon?"

"Look, ducks, why don't you just take the card to the doctor, tell him my ailment, and let him puzzle out the proper response."

She gazed at me with manifest disapproval for a long time. Then without a word got up and disappeared through a door behind the counter. In about thirty seconds she was back with her disapproval even more manifest and said icily, "The doctor will see you now." She was hoping for a prognosis of incurable. One of the ladies in the waiting room said something about the nerve of some people, and I slunk in through the doctor's door; no one likes a line bucker. Inside was a long corridor with examining rooms on either side. Croft stepped out of the last door on the right and said, "Come right in, Spenser. Good to see you again."

I went in and sat down in the patient's chair in front of Croft's big reassuring desk. On the wall was a big reassuring medical school diploma in Latin and several official-looking reassuring documents with state seals and such on them. Croft had a white medical coat over his wide-striped blue shirt and striped tie. He rested his elbows on the desk and cathedraled his hands in front of him with the tips of his fingers touching the bottom of his chin. He had a gold ring with a blue stone on the little finger of his left hand.

"How can I help you?" he asked and gave me his big predator's smile. Consoling. Reassuring. Phooey.

"Fraser Robinson tells me you are pimping for Vic Harroway." Croft didn't move except for the big smile. It went away. He said, "I beg your pardon?"

I said, "Knock it off, Croft. I've got you. I caught Robinson in a motel with an adolescent girl, and he confided in me. It doesn't have to be a long fall for you; I'm not with the AMA. Or the Vice Squad. You want to supplement your income by pimping while you heal, that's your doing. But I want to know everything you know about Harroway and Kevin Bartlett and how Earl Maguire got his neck broken and that kind of thing."

Croft reached over and pushed the intercom switch. "Joan," he said into it, "I can't be disturbed for at least a half hour. If an emergency comes up, switch it to Doctor LeBlac." He turned back toward me. "This is a mountain out of a molehill, Spenser."

"Yeah, I'll bet it is," I said.

"It is, in fact. Robinson is oversexed, and he's married to a woman who is undersexed. Nothing pathological, but it was making their marriage an armed camp. He came to me for help. You'd be surprised how many people come to their family doctor in time of trouble."

I said, "Cue the organ." Croft paid no attention.

"Fraser is not only a patient, he's a friend. Most of my patients are friends too. It's not all injections and take-these-pills-three-times-a-day. A lot of any family doctor's task is counseling, sometimes just being a guy that will listen."

"You may replace Rex Morgan as my medical idol, Doctor."

"I know, Spenser, you're a smart aleck, but the practice of medicine doesn't come out of textbook. Fraser needed an outlet, a chance for sexual adventure, and I gave it to him. It has saved his marriage, and I would do it again in a moment."

"How'd you happen to know about Harroway, Doctor?"

"I'd heard about him in town. Being a doctor in a town this size, the word gets around; you hear things."

"You ever meet him?"

"Of course not. We hardly move in the same circles." Croft looked at me steadily.

Candid. A modern Hippocrates.

"How'd you happen to have a card with his phone number on it?"

Croft's eyes faltered, only for a minute. "Card? I've never had a card for Harroway." He dropped his hands toward the middle drawer of his desk, then caught himself and folded them in his lap and leaned back in his chair.

"Yeah you did, and you gave it to Robinson—a little white card with a phone number printed on it and nothing else." I got up and walked past the desk to look out the window. It afforded a nice view of Route 128. Two small kids were sliding down the grassy embankment away from the highway using big pieces of cardboard for sleds. I turned around suddenly and pulled the middle drawer open. He tried to jam it shut, but I was stronger. In one corner was a neat stack of little white cards just like the one Robinson had given me. I took one out and stepped back away from the desk and sat down. Croft's face was red, and two deep lines ran from his Arabian nostrils to the corners of his mouth. I held the card in my right hand and snapped the edge of it with the ball of my thumb. It was very noisy in the quiet office.

He regrouped. "Well, naturally, it's not the kind of thing you admit. But I ran into Harroway once or twice at a pub on the highway and one thing led to another and I spent an evening with one of the girls from his house. Afterward,

Harroway asked me to take a few of these cards and give them to any of my patients who might be in, ah, the situation that Fraser was in."

"Croft," I said, "I am getting sort of mad. You are bullshitting me. A little discreet business card, printed up with just a phone number on it, for the sexually dysfunctional? Harroway? Harroway's idea of a subtle pander would be to stand on the corner near the Fargo Building yelling, *'Hey sailor, you want to get laid?'* You thought of this, and you're in it like an olive in a martini."

"You can't prove that."

"I can prove that. The point is you don't want me to. If I have to prove it, you'll be giving enemas at Walpole for the next five to ten. Now we can get around that, but not till you've spoken to me the words I'm longing to hear."

"What do you want?" Croft said. "What do you want me to tell you?"

"Where's Kevin Bartlett?"

"He's with Vic, in Boston. Vic's got an apartment in there on the Fenway."

"Address?"

"I don't know."

"You supply Harroway with drugs?"

"Absolutely not." He wasn't admitting what I hadn't proved.

"He ever give you money?"

"Never." The firmness of his denials seemed to give him confidence. He denied it again. "Never."

"Silly old me. I thought two nights ago by the bandstand on the Boston Common that you gave him a briefcase full of Quads and he gave you an envelope full of money." Croft looked as if his stomach hurt. "Probably not that at all though, huh? Probably buying your collection of Kay

Kayser records so he and the gang out at the house could have a sock hop. That what it was?"

Croft looked at the window and then the door and then at me. None of us helped him. He opened his mouth and closed it again. He rubbed both hands, palms down, along the arms of his chair. "I want a lawyer," he said. The words came out in a half croak.

"Now that's dumb," I said. "I mean, I might let you off the hook on this if you help me find the kid. But if you get a lawyer, then all this is going to come out, and maybe you'll end up being accessory to murder. You know how that'll cut into a guy's practice."

"I told you everything I know about the boy. He's with Vic in Boston."

"I need an address, and you have one. You're too much involved with Harroway not to know. You give me the address and maybe I can keep you out of the rest."

"On the Fenway. One-thirty-six Park Drive, Apartment Three."

I reached across the desk, picked up Croft's phone, and dialed. His eyes widened. "What are you going to do?" he said.

"I'm going to keep you on ice for a while." A voice answered, "Essex County Court House." I said, "Lieutenant Healy, please."

Croft started up from his seat. I reached over and pushed him back down with my hand on his shoulder. "Be cool," I said. "I can't trust you not to warn Harroway. If I get the kid back okay, I'll spring you."

Healy came on. I said, "This is Spenser. I got a suspect on the Bartlett kidnapping, or whatever."

Healy said, "Or whatever."

"And I want to put a lid on him for the afternoon so I can find the kid."

Healy said, "What's his name?"

"John Doe."

"Oh," Healy said. "Him."

"He gave me a lead on the kid, Lieutenant, and I've got to be sure he doesn't tip him off before I get there."

"I gather he didn't volunteer the lead."

"We practiced the art of compromise."

"And you want me to bury him someplace without a charge till you get the Bartlett kid, is that right?"

"Yeah."

"That is unconstitutional."

"Yeah."

"You think you'll lose the kid if you turn your back on John Doe?"

"Yeah." Croft was sitting perfectly still now, not looking at anything. There was a pause at Healy's end of the line. Then he said, "Okay. Where are you? I'll have one of the road patrols in your area pick him up."

"We'll be parked in the northbound lane of 128 under the Route 1 overpass. Red nineteen-sixty-eight Chevy convertible. Mass. plates seven-one-two-dash-two-three-four. If you need to contact me, call me here." I gave him Susan's number.

Healy said, "If this backfires, Spenser, I'll have your license and your ass." and hung up.

I said, "Okay, Doc. You get the picture. Let's go."

"How long will they hold me?"

"Till I get the kid. When he's home I'll come by and get you out."

"How will you know where I am?"

"Healy will know."

"Who is Healy?"

"State cop, works out of the Essex County DA's office.

Don't offer him money. He will deviate your septum if you do."

Croft called his girl again on the intercom, told her there was an emergency and he'd be gone for the day. We went out the back door of the office building and were parked under the Route 1 overpass when a blue State Police cruiser pulled up behind us and a tall red-haired state cop with big ears got out and came around to the driver's side of my car.

"You Spenser?" he said.

"Yep."

"I'm supposed to pick up a Mr. Doe," he said with no expression on his face.

I nodded at Croft. The trooper went around and opened the door. Croft got out. The trooper closed the door. I drove away.

24

The light blue Smithfield cruiser was still parked in the Bartletts' driveway, and Silveria, the bushy-haired cop, was reading a copy of *Sports Illustrated* in the front seat.

I parked beside him in the turnaround, and he looked at me over the top of the magazine as I got out. "Better not park that thing on the street on trash day," he said.

"Don't your lips get tired when you read?" I said.

"Your ears are gonna be tired when Mrs. Bartlett gets talking to you. She's been calling you things I don't understand."

"I gather no one tried to do her in."

"I think her husband might, and I wouldn't blame him. Jesus, what a mouth on that broad."

"Watch me soothe her with my silver tongue," I said.

Silveria said, "Good luck."

Marge Bartlett opened the back door and said, "Spenser, where in hell have you been, you rotten bastard?"

Silveria said, "Good, you've already got her half won over."

At the door I said to her, "I know where your son is."

She said, "We're paying you to protect me and you run off on your damned own."

I said, "I know where your son is, and I want your husband and you to come with me to get him."

She said, "It's lucky I'm alive."

I pushed past her into the house and said, "Where's your husband? Working today?"

She said, "Damn you, Spenser, aren't you going to explain yourself."

I went to the sink, filled a glass with water, turned back to her. She said, "I want a goddamned explanation." I poured the water on her head. She screamed and stepped back. She opened her mouth but nothing came out. The relief was wonderful.

"Now," I said. "I want you to listen to me, or I will get you so wet your skin will wrinkle." She pulled a paper towel from its roller under a cabinet and dried her hair. "I know where Kevin is. I want you and your husband to come with me to Boston and get him back."

"Can't you get him? I mean, won't there be trouble? I'm not even dressed. My hair's a mess. Mightn't it be better if you got him and brought him here? I mean, with me there he might make a scene."

"No," I said. "I'll locate him. And I'll take care of any trouble. But he's your kid. You bring him home. I won't drag him home for you. You owe him that."

"My husband is working in town—Arden Estates—he's putting up half a dozen houses near the Wakefield line on Salem Street. We can stop for him on the way."

"Okay," I said, "let's go. We'll take my car."

"I have to change," she said, "and put on my face and do something with my hair. I can't go out like this." She had on jeans and sneakers and a man's white shirt. The curls on each side of her face were held in place by Scotch Tape.

"We are not going out dancing to the syncopated rhythms of Blue Barron," I said.

She said, "I can't leave the house looking like this," and went upstairs. Twenty minutes later she descended in a double-breasted blue pinstripe pants suit with a blue and white polka-dot shirt and three-inch blue platform shoes. She had on lipstick, rouge, eye makeup, earrings, and doubtless much more that I didn't recognize. Her hair was stiff with spray. She put on big round blue-colored sunglasses, got her purse from the table in the front hall, and said she was ready.

I said, "I hope you got on clean underwear so if we get in an accident." She didn't answer me. And I left it at that. As long as she was quiet, I didn't want to press my luck.

When we found him at the construction trailer, Roger Bartlett was wearing green twill work clothes and carrying a clipboard.

"Hey," he said when I told him, "hey, that's great. Wait a minute, I'll tell the foreman and I'll be with you. Hey, that's okay." He went across the bulldozed road to a half-framed house and yelled up to one of the men on a scaffold. Then he put the clipbord down on the subfloor of the house and came to my car.

"Get in back, Roger, would you? It's hard for me without wrinkling my suit."

She leaned forward and held the seat, and he slid into the back.

On the ride in I told them a little of what I knew. I didn't mention Croft or Fraser Robinson. I merely told them that I had an address in town where Kevin was staying, and I knew he was staying with Vic Harroway. Neither Bartlett nor his wife knew Harroway. "The sonova bitch," Bartlett said, "if he's hurt my kid, I'll kill him."

"No," I said. "You let me handle Harroway. He is not easy. You stay away from him."

"He's got my kid, not yours," Bartlett said.

"He hasn't harmed Kevin. They like one another. Kevin's with him by choice."

Bartlett said, "The sonova bitch."

We drove along Storrow Drive with the river on our right, took the Kenmore exit, went up over Commonwealth Avenue and onto Park Drive. On the right, apartment houses in red brick and yellow brick, most of them built probably before the war, some with courtyards, low buildings, no more than five stories. It was a neighborhood of graduate students and retired school teachers and middle-aged couples without children. On the left, following the curve of the muddy river, was the Fenway. In early fall it was still bright with flowers, the trees were still dominantly green, and the reeds along the river were higher than a man. Whenever I passed them, I expected Marlin Perkins to jump out and sell me some insurance.

Number 136 was three quarters of the way down Park Drive, across from the football field. At that point the drive was divided by a broad grass safety island, and I pulled my car up onto it and parked.

Marge Bartlett said, "It's not a bad neighborhood. Look, it's across the street from the museum. And there's a nice park."

"Breeding shows," I said. We went across the street and rang the bell marked Super. A fat middle-aged woman with no teeth and gray hair in loose disorganization around her head shuffled to the door. She was wearing fluffy pink slippers and a flowered housedress. When she opened the door, I showed her a badge that said "Suburban Security Service" on it and said in a mean vice-squad voice, "Where's Apartment Three?"

She said, "Right there on the left, officer, first door. What's the trouble?"

"No trouble," I said, "just routine."

I knocked on the door with the Bartletts right behind me. No answer. I knocked again then put my ear against the panel. Silence. "Open it," I said to the super.

"I don't know," she said, "I mean the tenants get mad if . . ."

"Look, sweetheart," I said, "if I have to come back here with a warrant, I might bring along someone from the Building Inspector's office. And we might go over this roach farm very closely, you know."

"Okay, okay, no need to get mad. Here." She produced a key ring and opened the door. I went in with my hand on my gun. It was not a distinguished place. Two rooms, kitchen and bath off a central foyer that was painted a dull pink. The place was neat. The bed was made. There was a pound of frozen hamburg half-defrosted on the counter. In the bedroom there were twin beds. On each were some clothes.

Roger Bartlett looked at a pair of flared jeans and a pale blue polo shirt and said, "Those are Kevin's." On the other bed was a pair of Black Watch plaid trousers with deep cuffs, and a forest-green silk short-sleeved shirt with a button-down collar. A pair of stacked-heel black loafers was on the floor beside the bed. On the bureau there was a framed eight-by-ten color photo of Harroway and the boy. Harroway had an arm draped over the boy's shoulders, and they were both smiling.

Two spots of color showed on Roger Bartlett's face as he looked at the picture.

"This the guy?" he said.

"That's him."

"He's really quite nice-looking in a physical sort of way," Marge Bartlett said. "The apartment is quite neat too." Her husband looked at her, opened his mouth, and then closed it.

"Let's go," I said. And we trailed out. The super came

last in line to make sure we didn't lift anything and closed the door behind her. I said, "Okay for now. If you run into Mr. Harroway, say nothing. This is official business, and it's to be kept still." I thought about invoking national security, but she might get suspicious.

"What now?" Bartlett said when we got outside again.

"We wait," I said. "Obviously they'll be coming back. Clothes laid out on the bed, hamburg defrosting for supper." We walked back toward my car when Marge Bartlett said, "My God, it's Kevin."

25

On the far side of the Fenway two figures were jogging. One big man, one small one. Vic and Kevin. Harroway was taking it easy, and the boy was obviously straining to stay with him. Cross streets made a natural circle of that part of the Fenway, and one complete lap around it, without crossing any streets, was about a mile. If we stayed where we were, Harroway and the boy would run right up to us. We walked across to the park and stood, partly shielded by a blue hydrangea, watching them. As they got closer, you could see Harroway talking, apparently encouragingly, to Kevin, who had his head down, jogging doggedly. Harroway had on a lavender net sleeveless shirt and blue sweat pants with zippers at the ankles and white stripes down the sides. Kevin had on a white T-shirt and gray sweat pants, a little big and obviously brand-new. The boy was breathing hard, and Harroway said, "Just to the edge of the stands, Kev; that's a mile. Then we'll walk a bit. You can make it. You're doing terrific." Behind us, along the near sideline of the football field, cement stands descended maybe twenty feet below street level to the field.

Roger Bartlett stepped forward and said, "Kevin." The boy saw him and without a word he veered left, jumped the low back of the grandstand, and ran down the cement stands. Bartlett went after him. Marge Bartlett began to scream after them, "Kevin, you come back here. Kevin." I was watching Harroway. He looked at me a long ten seconds, then looked after the boy. Bartlett was gaining on his son rapidly. The boy was bushed from jogging. Bartlett caught the boy in midfield, and Harroway went after them. I said, "Stay here," to Marge Bartlett and went after Harroway. Bartlett had Kevin by the arm, and the boy was struggling and punching at his father with his free hand.

"Let me go, you sonova bitchin' bastard," Kevin said.

"Kevin, Kevin, I want us to go home," Bartlett said. He was crying.

Harroway got there ahead of me. He caught a handful of the back of Bartlett's work shirt and threw him sprawling toward the end zone.

"I want to stay with you, Vic." Kevin was crying too now, and behind me I could hear Marge Bartlett begin to wail. Jesus. Maybe I should get out of this line of work. Get into something simple and clean. Maybe a used-car salesman. Politics. Loan sharking.

Harroway said, "No one's taking you anywhere, Kev. No one."

Bartlett came up on his feet, the red spots on his cheekbones much brighter now. "Stay out of this, Spenser," he said. "That's my kid."

Harroway's arms and shoulders gleamed with sweat, and the afternoon sun made glistening highlights on the deltoid muscles that draped over his incredible shoulders.

"Bartlett," I said, "don't be crazy."

"Let him try it," Kevin said. "No one can beat Vic. All of you together can't beat Vic. Go ahead, Roger." The first name dripped with distaste. "Let's see you try to handle Vic."

Bartlett did. He must have been nearly fifty and probably hadn't had a fight since World War II. He was a wiry man

and had worked with his hands all his life, but compared to
Harroway he was one of the daughters of the poor. He ran at
Harroway with his head down. Harroway caught him by the
shirt front with his left hand and clubbed him across the face
with his right. Twice. Then he let him go, and Bartlett fell.
He tried to get up, couldn't, caught hold of Harroway's leg,
and tried to pull him down. Harroway didn't move.

"Okay," I said and reached back for my gun, "that's
. . . ." and Marge Bartlett jumped at Harroway, still
wailing, and swung at him with both clenched fists. He
swatted her away from him with the back of his right hand,
and she sprawled in the mud on her back. Told her to stay up
there. There was blood showing from her nose. Kevin said,
"Mama."

I had the gun out now and held it by my side. "Enough,"
I said. Bartlett was oblivious. All he had left was going into
bending Harroway's leg, and he might as well have been
working on a hydrant.

Harroway said, "Get him off me or I'll kick him into the
river."

I stepped closer with the gun still at my side and pulled
Bartlett away by the collar. Marge Bartlett was sitting on her
heels with her head back trying to stop her nose from
bleeding. Bartlett sat on the ground and looked at Harroway. Harroway had his arm around Kevin's shoulder.

"He's staying with me," Harroway said.

I held the gun up and said, "We'll have to see about
that."

"No," Harroway said. "We won't see. He's staying with
me. I don't care about your goddamned gun."

"That's the only way you can get me," Kevin said, "if
you use a gun. You don't dare try and stop Vic by yourself.
Nobody does. Nobody can. We're staying together. If you

try to shoot him, you'll have to shoot me first." The kid moved between Harroway and me.

Marge Bartlett said, "Kevin, you stop that right now. You are coming home with us. Now don't be ridiculous."

Kevin didn't look at her. "You see what he did to Big Rog." I could feel the distaste like a force. I wondered how his father must feel. "He'll do that to anyone that bothers me. He takes care of me. We take care of each other." The kid had big dark eyes, and on his cheeks, just like his father's, two bright spots of color showed.

I flipped the cylinder open on my gun and, with the barrel pointing up, shook the bullets out into my left hand. I put the bullets in my pants pocket, put the gun in my holster. Then I took off my jacket, folded it, and put it on the ground. I unclipped my holster and put it on the jacket.

Kevin said, "What are you doing?"

I said, "I'm going to beat your man."

Marge Bartlett said, "Spenser," in a strained voice. Harroway smiled.

"I'm going to beat your man, Kevin, so you'll know it can be done. Then I'm going to let you decide."

Marge Bartlett said, "He can't decide. He's not old enough." No one paid any attention. Harroway gently took Kevin's shoulders and moved him out of the way. "Watch this, Kev. It won't take long." He shrugged his shoulders forward, and the triceps swelled out at the back of his upper arms. "Come and get it, Spenser."

I wasn't paying attention to his arms. I was watching his feet. If he set up as if he knew what he was doing, I might be in some trouble. We both knew I couldn't outmuscle him. He stood with his feet spread, flat-footed in a slight crouch. Good. He didn't know what he was doing. Sometimes an iron freak will get hung up on karate and kung fu, or sometimes they're wrestlers. Harroway was none of those. If I could keep my concentration, and if he didn't get hold of me, I had him.

I shuffled toward him. The ground was dry and firm. I had a lot of room. We were in the middle of the football field. A few people had begun to gather in along the sidewalk and a couple in the stands. They were uneasy, looking at the trouble. We who are about to die salute you. I was dressed for the work; I had on sneakers and Levi's jeans, my stakeout clothes. I put a left jab on Harroway's nose. He grabbed at me, and I moved out. Float like a butterfly, sting like a bee. Come to think of it, he wasn't champ anymore, was he? Harroway swung on me with his right hand. Better and better. I let it go by, stepped in behind it, and drove two hard right-hand punches into his kidneys; hitting the muscle web of the latissimus dorsi under his rib cage was like hitting a chain link fence. I moved back away from him. He grazed me with his left fist, and I hit him in the nose again. It started to bleed. I hoped Marge Bartlett was pleased. The silence in the open field seemed thunderous. The sound of a helicopter, probably one of the traffic reporters, made the silence seem more thunderous by contrast. The helicopter bothered my concentration. Watch his middle, watch his feet, let peripheral vision take care of his fists, he can't fake with his middle. Stay away. Don't let him get hold of you. I tried a combination. Left jab, left hook, right cross. It worked. I scored on all three. But no one was counting. Harry Balleau wasn't going to jump into the ring at the end and raise my hand. If we clinched, Artie Donovan wasn't going to jump in and make sure we broke clean. There was a mouse starting under Harroway's right eye. I circled him counterclockwise. Moving my hands in front of me, shuffling, keeping my left foot forward. Don't get caught walking. Don't let him get you between steps. Shuffle, jab, one two, shuffle, jab, one two. Move in. Move

out. I was way ahead on points. But Harroway didn't seem
to be weakening. He lunged at me. I moved out of the way
and got him with the side of my fist on the temple. Don't
break your hand. Don't hit his head with your knuckles.
Shuffle, move. Jab. The sweat began to slip down my chest
and arms; it felt good. I was getting looser and quicker.
Ought to warm up really. Should do some squat jumps and
stretching exercises before you have a fight with a 215-
pound body builder who probably killed a guy with his fist
last week. Harroway was breathing a little short. I gave him
a dip with my right shoulder, went left, and dug my left fist
into his stomach. He grunted. He got hold of my shoulder
with his left hand. I twisted in toward him and came up
under his jaw with the heel of my right hand. His head
jolted back. I hammered him in the Adam's apple with the
edge of the same hand. He made a choking sound. I rolled
on out away from him, breaking the grip on my shoulder as
I did, and brought my left elbow back against his cheekbone
with the full weight of my rolling 195 behind it. He went
down. I heard Kevin gasp. Harroway was halfway up when
I finished my roll and kicked him in the face. I sprawled him
over on his side. He kept going, rolled over, and came up.
Maybe I was just making him mad. There was a lot of blood
on his face and shirt now. Besides his nose, there was a cut
under the eye where the mouse had been. The eye was
almost closed. The right side of his face where my elbow
had caught him was beginning to puff. He seemed to have
trouble breathing. I wondered if I'd broken something in the
neck. He came at me. I went to work on the other eye. Two
jabs, a left hook. Move away, circle. Concentrate. Don't let
him grab you. Don't let him tag you. Concentrate. Move.
Jab. He swung a right roundhouse, and I caught it on my
forearm. The whole arm went numb, and I backpedaled out
of range waiting for it to recover. Better not let that happen

again. Harroway kept coming. His face was bloody. One eye was shut and the other closing. His breathing was hoarse and labored, but he kept coming on. I felt a tickle of fear in my stomach. What if I couldn't stop him? Never mind what if I couldn't. Think about jabbing and moving. Concentrate. Don't think things that don't help. Don't think at all. Concentrate. I jabbed the closing eye. Harroway grunted in pain. He was having trouble seeing. I hit the same eye again. There was a cut on the eyebrow, and the blood was blinding him. He stood still. Weaving a little. Like a buffalo, with his head lowered. I stepped away from him.

"Stop it, Harroway," I said.

He shook his head and lunged toward the sound of my voice. I moved away and hit him a left hook in the neck.

"Stop it, you goddamned fool," I said.

He came at me again. I stepped in toward him like a lineman on a pass rush and came up against the side of his head with my forearm, my whole body behind it, driving off my legs. Harroway straightened up and fell over on his back without a sound. The shock of the impact tingled the length of my arm and up into my shoulder. No one said anything. Kevin stood by himself opposite his mother and father, with Harroway between them lying on his back in the sun.

Kevin said, "Don't, Vic. Get up. Don't quit. Don't let him beat you. Don't quit."

"He didn't quit, kid, he's hurt. Anybody can be hurt."

"He let you beat him."

"No. He couldn't stop me. But there's no shame in that. It's just something I know how to do better than he does. He's a man, kid. I think he's a no-good sonova bitch. But he didn't quit. He went as far as he could, for you. In fact he went a lot farther than he could, for you. So did your mother and father."

Now that it was over I was shaky. My shirt was soaked with sweat. My arms trembled and my legs felt weak. I took the bullets out of my pants pocket and reloaded the gun while I talked. "How far have you gone for anybody lately?"

The boy still looked at Harroway. In the distance I heard a siren. Somebody had called for the buzzers, and here they came. Kevin started to cry. He stood looking at Harroway and cried with his hands straight down by his side.

"I don't know what to do," he said. Roger Bartlett got his feet under him and stood up. He put out his hand and helped his wife up. He fumbled a handkerchief out of his hip pocket and gave it to her, and she held it against her still-leaky nose. The two of them stood looking at Kevin who stood crying. Then Marge Bartlett said, "Oh, honey," and stepped over Harroway and put her arms around the kid and cried too. Then Bartlett got his arms around both of them and held on for dear life. Harroway sat up, painfully, and hugged his knees and looked at me with his one slightly open eye.

"Slut?" I said. He looked at me without comprehension. I said, "A couple of days ago you called Susan Silverman a slut." He still looked blank. "Never mind," I said.

26

It was suppertime before we got things cleaned up with the
Boston cops and I got back to Smithfield. Boston would
hold Harroway on an assault charge until they straightened
out with Healy and Trask the kidnapping, murder, extortion,
contributing to the delinquency of a minor, and procuring
charges that seemed likely. Kevin went home with his
mother and father, and I went to Susan Silverman's house to
see if there was any cassoulet or champagne or whatever left
around and to soak my hands in ice water. She gave me
bourbon on the rocks with a dash of bitters in a big glass.
We sat on her couch.

"And was it Vic Harroway all along?" she said.

"Nope, not entirely. According to Harroway it was
actually Croft that ran things. He got them drugs, set up the
prostitution customers, kept things cool with the local
fuzz."

"Chief Trask?"

"Maybe. Harroway says he doesn't know. He knows
only that Croft said the cops wouldn't bother him."

"Did he kill Maguire?"

"Yeah. Harroway says it was an accident. He and Kevin
were going to get some of Kevin's things. Harroway was
lifting some booze while they were at it, and Maguire

194

caught them. Maguire panicked, grabbed for the poker, and Harroway hit him too hard."

"And the kidnapping and the sick jokes and everything?"

"That's not too clear. Harroway seemed to have two reasons. First, practical: he thought that they could finance 'a new life together'—that's what he called it—by putting the arm on the old man for the ransom money. And he says then he thought once they got the dough that they'd have a little sport with the straight world. Kevin says it was his idea, but Harroway says no, it was all his own doing. He also says that Kevin was upstairs in his room when Maguire got killed, but Kevin says he was there. Harroway seems to be protecting him, and Kevin's not entirely coherent. You can imagine. He's torn apart. He found out he still had some feelings for his mother and father he didn't realize he had, and it's all over for Harroway, and the kid knows it."

Susan said, "I wonder if it was good or bad for him to see Harroway beaten."

"I thought it would be good. I hope I was right. Harroway represented something solid and safe and inde-structible; you know, a kind of fantasy superhero to insulate Kevin from the world, to be everything his father wasn't and his mother wouldn't let him or his father be."

"Maybe," she said. "Or maybe it's a glib generalization that won't hold. I guess we'll have to wait awhile and see how therapy works. Psychological truth usually isn't that neat."

"Yeah," I said, "but I didn't have time to wait and see out there in the field."

She said, "I know. You do what you have to. And besides, he insulted us once, didn't he?"

"Yeah," I said, "there's that."

I rattled the empty glass at her, and she got up and refilled it. The bourbon made a spread of warmth in my stomach. I took my left hand out of the ice water and put my right one in. I put my feet up on the coffee table and rested my head on the back of her couch. Susan came back with the second drink.

"You know," I said, "he was a nasty, brutish, mean sonova bitch. But he loved that kid."

"They all do," Susan Silverman said.

"You mean his mother and father?" She nodded. "Yeah, you're right," I said, "they do. You should have seen that henpecked, browbeaten bastard try to go up against Harroway. You've seen what Harroway looks like, and Bartlett tried to take him. And so did she. Amazing." I took my right hand out of the ice water and switched my glass to it and put my left arm around Susan's shoulder.

She said, "How did Croft and Harroway get mixed up together?"

"Harroway says that Croft looked him up. Harroway was doing a little bit of small-time pimping, and he says Croft told him he knew all about it and had an idea for them to get a much bigger and more profitable operation. He'd supply the drugs, get the word around, and Harroway would do the on-the-spot managerial duties."

"And they split?"

"No, that's the interesting part. Harroway says Croft had a silent partner. Harroway never knew who it was. One third of the take was a lot more dough than Harroway ever dreamed of, and he didn't complain."

"Do we know the silent partner?"

I shook my head. "I imagine Healy will get that out of Croft in a while."

"Oh, speaking of Healy, there's a message here for you from him. And one from some policeman in Boston." She went to the kitchen and came back with an envelope which said New England Telephone in the return address space.

She looked at it and said, "A woman called—I didn't get her name—and said she was from Lieutenant Healy's office, and the Lieutenant wanted you to know that the package you gave him to keep is being stored at the Smithfield Police Station. You can pick it up when you need it, but it better be soon."

"That's Croft," I said. "They must have gotten nervous riding him around and figured to let Trask bear the brunt of a false arrest suit."

"And," she said, "I have a message that you should call either a Sergeant Belson or a Lieutenant Quirk when you came in. They said you knew the number."

"Do I ever," he said. "Okay. I'll do that now." I hated to get up, and I was beginning to get stiff. Ten years ago I didn't get stiff this soon. I let my feet down off the coffee table and drank most of the second bourbon and got myself upright. I felt as if I needed a lube job. A few more bourbons and I'd be oiled. Ah, Spenser, your wit's as keen as ever. I dialed Boston Homicide and got Quirk.

"I got the information on your man," he said. No salutation, no golly, Spenser, it's swell to hear your voice. Sometimes I wasn't sure how fond Quirk was of me.

"Okay," I said.

"He's got a record. Wanted in Tacoma, Washington, for performing an illegal abortion. Got himself disbarred or delicensed or whatever the hell they do with doctors that screw up. That was about seven years ago. Now he could probably do it legal in half the country, but then it was still a big unh-unh."

"And he's still wanted?"

"Yeah, he skipped bail and disappeared. The AG's office out there has an outstanding warrant on him, but it's not international intrigue. I don't think there are a lot of people working on it these days."

"Anything else?"

"Nothing much. Seems the guy had a good practice before this happened. I met the homicide commander out there once, and I gave him a call. Says this Croft was well thought of. Probably did the abortion as a kindness, not for dough. Didn't want to be quoted, but said he thought it was kind of a shafting. Girl's old man made a goddamned crusade of it, you know?"

"Yeah."

"One thing, though," Quirk said.

"What's that?"

"Yours isn't the first inquiry on him. Chief Trask of the Smithfield Police checked on him six years ago. There's a Xerox copy of Trask's request and a Xerox copy of the report the ID Bureau sent him."

"Six years ago?" I said. Something bad was nudging at me.

"Yeah, what's going on out there? Nice to see you're in close touch with the local law enforcement agencies."

I said, "Jesus Christ."

Quirk said, "What?"

I said, "I'll get back to you," and hung up.

Susan said, "What's the matter?"

I said, "I'll be back," and headed for my car. It was about five minutes from Susan's house to the Smithfield jail. "Trask," I said out loud, "that sonova bitch." I slammed the car into the parking lot in front of the town hall and ran for the police station. Fire, police, and town hall were connected in a brick-faced white-spired town hall complex. The police station was in the middle between the double-doored fire station and the church-fronted town hall. Like a breezeway, I thought as I went in.

Trask was at the desk. I didn't like that. The chief

shouldn't do desk duty. He looked up as I came in. "Well, Spenser," he said, "solve everything?"

I said, "Where's Croft?"

Trask jerked his head toward a door behind the desk. "Down there in a cell, safe and sound."

"I want to see him."

Trask was friendly, positively jolly. My stomach felt tight. I didn't want to go down and see Croft. "Sure," Trask said. He swiveled his chair around and snapped the bolt back on the door. "Third cell," he said. And opened the door.

There was a short corridor with three barred cells along the left side and a blank cinder block wall along the right. The first two cells were empty. In the third one Dr. Croft was hanging from the highest bar with his swollen tongue sticking out and his blank eyes popped way out. He was dead. I felt the nausea start up my throat, and it took me about thirty seconds to swallow it back. His red and silver rep striped necktie was knotted around his neck and around the top cross member in the barred door. I knew he was dead even before I reached my hand through to feel his pulse. I also knew I had something to do with it. I went back down the corridor and closed the door behind me. Trask had his feet up on an open desk drawer and was reading a mimeographed sheet of paper. He was wearing glasses. His thick red neck was smoothly shaved where his crew cut ended. He looked up as I closed the door.

"Everything okay down there?" he said. The glasses distorted his small pale eyes when he looked at me.

I said, "How come you're doing desk duty, Chief?"

"Aw, hell, you know how a small department is. I mean, we only got twelve men. I like to give some of the kids a break. You know. I mean it ain't like I'm commissioner in

Boston or something." He smiled at me, a big friendly hick smile. He'd never liked me this well before.

There was a table along the wall to the left of the cell block door. It had chrome legs and a maple-colored Formica top. There was a coffee percolator plugged in on it and a half-empty box of paper cups. I took one and poured myself some coffee. Then I sat on the table facing Trask. The silent partner.

"Trask," I said, "I know you murdered Croft."

He never blinked. "What the hell are you talking about?" he said.

"No crap now, there's just the two of us here. You went down that corridor and tied that tie around his neck and hoisted him up there and let him strangle because he was the only link between you and Harroway and with him dead no one would have any way of finding out what you were into."

Trask looked straight at me and said, "What was I into?"

"You were into prostitution and narcotics and sex shows and probably can be arraigned for abusing a goat."

"You can't prove any of that."

"Not right now, I can't. But I know some things and I'm going to tell them to Healy and he's going to prove it."

"What do you know?"

"I know that you know that Croft is wanted in Tacoma, and that you knew it six years ago. Now that's not much for starters. But I bet if we start pulling on that little loose end, after a while there may be a whole weave we can ravel out. You learned that little bit of business, and you used it to blackmail Croft. Maybe you got suspicious of the way he just drifted in here; maybe he confided in you; I don't know. But I'll bet you had the whole cesspool all worked out in your head and were just waiting for a middleman. And plop, into your lap dropped Croft. So he dealt with

Harroway and you dealt with him. And nobody else knew anything about it. Until Harroway got a crush on a goddamned runaway and screwed up the whole thing."

Trask was still looking straight at me.

"And then you get Croft right in your own jail. Merry Christmas, from me and Healy. And you figured, okay, this is the only way they can get me. If he's gone, I'm safe. Did it bother you to strangle him like that with the necktie? Did he croak and kick trying to breathe? How you going to explain not taking his tie away from him?"

Trask kept looking without a word.

"I feel mean about it. I think Croft wasn't that bad a guy and he made a mistake that was motivated by a decent impulse and it destroyed him, and you used it to make him a goddamned pimp and then you killed him. I feel really mean about that part, you cold-blooded sonova bitch. Because I delivered him to you. And Healy will feel mean about it because he did too. And we will nail your ass for it. You can believe that. We only know a little, and we'll have to guess a lot, but we will have you for it."

Trask said, "Not if you don't tell anybody. It's a sweet setup. Or it was. I could pass on a few of the profits to you. Maybe you could even recruit a new manager for the girls and take Croft's job yourself. Or maybe we could cut out the middleman; you could combine the jobs. Maybe you don't have the drug contacts, but the girls are better revenue in this town anyway."

I leaned forward a little and spit in his face. He flushed red and the pearl-handled General Patton forty-five came out. "All right, smart guy. If you don't want coin, maybe there's another way." He wiped my saliva away with the back of his hand. His sun-bleached blond eyebrows looked white against his red face. "You come in here, tried to spring Croft, pulled a gun, I shot you in self-defense, and Croft sees it's no use hoping anymore and hangs himself."

I laughed. "Oh, good, even though the state cop who put him here told you to hold Croft for me. Even though I'm here five minutes after a Boston dick named Quirk tells me about your request for info on Croft six years ago. What a mammoth intellect you are, Trask. How the hell did you figure out this hustle by yourself anyway?"

Trask said, "Yeah, you think you're so goddamned smart; you'll be dead and I'll be gone and we'll see who's so goddamned smart then."

I threw the cup of coffee in his face and kicked the gun out of his hand. It went over the counter and skidded along the floor. Trask started to get up, and I was on my feet in front of him. "Go for it," I said. "Get up and try and get by me and go for the gun, you piece of garbage." He half rose from the chair and then sat down. "I'm not moving," he said.

I turned and walked away from him. At the door I picked up his gun. A Colt, single-action, six-inch barrel. I threw it through the glass front window.

"I'll be in touch with Healy," I said. "And he'll be in touch with you. Start running, you sonova bitch."

I walked out and left the door open behind me.

Here's one inning of Spenser's first major league game. You'll want to read the whole nine innings in MORTAL STAKES, now available from Dell.

It was drizzly rainy along the Charles. I ran along the esplanade with my mind on other things and it took a lot longer to do my three miles. It always does if you don't concentrate. I was on the curb by Arlington Street looking to dash across Storrow Drive and head home when a black Ford with a little antenna on the roof pulled alongside and Frank Belson stuck his head out the window on the passenger side and said, "Get in."

I got in the back seat and we pulled away. "Drive around for a while, Billy," Belson said to the other cop, and we headed west toward Allston.

Belson was leaning forward trying to light a cigar butt with the lighter from the dashboard. When he got it going, he shifted around, put his left arm on the back of the front seat and looked at me.

"I got a snitch tells me that Frank Doerr's going to blow you up."

"Frank personally?"

"That's what the snitch says. Says you roughed Frank up yesterday and he took it personally." Belson was thin, with tight skin and a dark beard shaved close. "Marty thought you oughta know."

We stayed left where the river curved and drove out Soldiers Field Road, past the 'BZ radio tower.

"I thought Wally Hogg did that kind of work for Doerr."

"He does," Belson said. "But this one he's gonna do himself."

"If he can," I said.

"That ain't to say he might not have Wally around to hold you still," Belson said.

Billy U-turned over the safety island and headed back in toward town. He was young and stylish with a thick blond mustache and a haircut that hid his ears. Belson's sideburns were trimmed at the temple.

"Reliable snitch?"

Belson nodded. "Always solid in the past."

"How much you pay him for this stuff?"

"C-note," Belson said.

"I'm flattered," I said.

Belson shrugged. "Company money," he said.

We were passing Harvard Stadium. "You or Quirk got any thoughts about what I should do next?"

Belson shook his head.

"How about hiding," Billy said. "Doerr will probably die in the next ten, twenty years."

"You think he's that tough?"

Billy shrugged. Belson said, "It's not tough so much. It's crazy. Doerr's crazy. Things don't work out, he wants to kill everybody. I hear he cut one guy up with a machete. I mean cut him up. Dis-goddamn-membered him. Crazy."

"You don't think a dozen roses and a note of apology would do it, huh?"

Billy snorted. Belson didn't bother. We passed the Kenmore exit.

I said to Billy, "You know where I live?"

He nodded.

Belson said, "You got a piece on you?"

"Not when I'm running," I said.

"Then don't run," Belson said. "If I was Doerr I coulda aced you right there at the curb when we picked you up."

I remembered my lecture to Lester about professionals. I had no comment. We swung off at Arlington and then right on Marlborough. Billy pulled up in front of my apartment.

"You're going up a one-way street," I said to Billy.

"Geez, I hope there's no cops around," Billy said.

I got out. "Thanks," I said to Belson.

He got out too. "I'll walk up to your place with you."

"With me? Frank, you old softy."

"Quirk told me to get you inside safe. After that you're on your own. We don't run a baby-sitting service. Not even for you, baby."

When I unlocked my apartment door, I noticed that Belson unbuttoned his coat. We went in. I looked around. The place was empty. Belson buttoned his coat.

"Watch your ass," he said, and left.